JACKED UP

JANE HENRY

JACKED UP (Hard n' Dirty)

Copyright 2018 by Jane Henry

Chapter One

Tanya

I PULL out my compact mirror and purse my lips, checking my makeup. Hair is in place, too-short dress wrinkle-free, just enough cleavage showing.

Eyes ready to go all puppy dog when the time is right.

I've spent two sleepless nights perusing the web, trying to find a classic car repair shop that could do what I need them to. This place, thank *God* only a short drive from my home in Manhattan, fits the bill. Reviewers say it's excellent, and they turn out top-quality work. The only bad reviews mention the repair shop owner and the shop itself. They say he's grumpy and irritable, and other reviews say the shop needs a good, thorough clean. So I've prepared myself: bottle of instant hand sanitizer in my purse, check. Black dress that won't show any stains if I come into contact with anything in the shop, check. Perfect smile in place so I can charm the grumpy owner, check.

My hands are sweaty, my stomach in knots. I've never

done anything like this in my life. Hell, I hardly even know how to park. I'm used to valets and escorts and rarely have to do something so… *normal*… as driving to a repair shop and parking my car. Yeah, maybe I've been a little sheltered.

It isn't the newness of the experience that makes me nervous, but how desperate I am for them to say yes, they'll help me.

I inhale deeply. Stand up tall. *Exude confidence and aplomb,* my mom told me. *Appearances are everything.* As soon as I could walk on two legs, she began teaching me how to walk with my shoulders pulled back, my spine straightened, like we were in some sort of marching band. I learned, though. How to walk with dignity, dress with pride, and present myself as Tanya Hayes, Daughter of Raymond and Sasha Hayes. Heiress to the Hayes Family Automotives Legacy.

I was kept out of the public eye as a child, hidden from the publicity and attention my father and mother received . The little princess. So fortunately, when I go about my business, people rarely know who I am. I'm not easily recognizable.

I'm hoping that's the case today. Hell, everything's sort of banking on it.

I grit my teeth as I walk on these killer heels to my destination. I see the shop from a distance, and recognize it immediately from the pictures I saw online. Gleaming chrome accents the window frames, enormous picture windows displaying a beautiful car in candy-apple red. It's all a little like I've stepped back in time, to a simpler place, like if I push open the doors to that shop I'll be able to sit on a stool and order a drink from an old-fashioned soda fountain.

The cars are all lined up, and these are not the little beaters and rusty, ancient things I saw at some other shops.

Jacked Up

These are the real deals. Mint condition. Exclusive. *Gorgeous*.

I have no idea what most of the names for the cars are. I don't *care* what the names are. All I care about is finding someone who can help me.

I push open the door and enter, forgetting my plan on being all put-together and professional. I can't help but wrinkle up my nose when the pungent scent of oil and grease fills my senses. It's pretty from the outside, but the reviews were right. The inside of this place needs some serious attention.

It's vacant in here, and I look around for some sort of bell or something I can ring to get someone's attention, but there's nothing. Against one wall is a glass display of books that catches my attention. Curious, I walk over and look at the titles. They're vintage covers featuring classic cars, but half of them look like pin-up posters with half-naked women gracing the cover. Interesting.

Another display case to the left houses miniature replicas of classic cars. I have to admit, they're beautiful. Canary yellow, robin's egg blue, and cherry red, black and silver with gleaming windshields. And the attention to detail astounds me. They're not behind the glass like the books, so I reach out and run a finger along one edge. As soon as my finger glides along the edge of a pretty black racecar, a door jangles open and I nearly jump out of my skin. I feel like a kid caught red-handed with her hand in the cookie jar. Something tells me I'm not supposed to touch these little cars. I swivel around and put my hands behind my back like I'm totally innocent. I'm not expecting what I see.

Behind me is a guy wiping his hands on a dirty rag. He stands behind the desk, but he's so tall and broad I can see him clearly. He's got dark brown, longish hair slicked back, and a thick, dark beard. He's wearing a short-sleeved black t-shirt that stretches tight against his chest, revealing muscled arms completely covered in tattoos. I don't want to stare, so I only look quickly. There are skulls and flowers, the flowers being the only color in a sea of black. His eyes pierce me in place with a stern but curious look, and an instant throb pulses low in my belly.

My pulse quickens. He's got an immediate vibe of danger. My breath catches.

Day-*um*.

He's not my type. He's *so* not my type.

Then why do I feel all nervous and lightheaded? Why are my palms sweaty? My heart tip-taps a crazy beat.

"Hi," I say as cheerfully as I can, swallowing hard. "I'm looking for the owner of this shop." This has to be one of the guys who works for him. This man doesn't *look* like the crotchety owner described in those reviews online. The owner has to be old and gray and grumpy.

Hellllo, stranger.

The man finishes wiping his hands and places the rag on the top. "Alright," he says. His voice is deep and growly like he gargles with whiskey and cigarettes, but his eyes twinkle a little. "When I fetch him, who do I say's askin' for him?"

"I—please tell him—Felicia is here," I stammer, totally unprepared for this. My voice sounds weirdly high-pitched and squeaky because I'm a terrible liar, but he can't know my real name. He cocks a brow at me that's more than curious. There's an undercurrent of correction in it that makes my throat tighten. He knows. God, I'm *awful* at lying.

"Got it," he says, his eyes shuttering. I must've imagined a spark of friendliness there. His jaw clenches and his lip thin as he pushes the rag on the counter and goes into the shop. I gasp for a breath I didn't even know I was holding. The door jangles with a bell and shuts behind him with an ominous *click*.

The minutes tick by. Where the hell is he? I glance nervously at my phone, but it doesn't give me any answers. Did I make a mistake coming here? *God.* I straighten out my skirt and look longingly at the line-up of the replicas. I want to touch them again.

Seconds turn into minutes. Easily ten minutes later, the door to the shop opens, and the same guy walks in. I look at him quizzically. Where's the owner? I'm growing impatient now. I have things to do, and this is a waste of my time. He walks over to me and extends his hand. What the hell? I stare and finally take his hand. It's rough, large, and warm. I swallow hard.

"Nice to meet you, Felicia," he says, though his voice is rough and tight. He's anything but pleased to meet me, and that gets my hackles up. Has he already judged me?

"What brings you here?" he asks.

"I was hoping to meet the owner," I say through tight lips. "I need to speak to him regarding a very important matter. Crucial, really, and extremely time-sensitive."

He releases my hand to cross his arms on his chest, making his biceps bulge. I swear to God the skull tattoo is glaring right at me, like some sort of omen. Is that why he has it? I blink and try to keep calm.

"Name's Levi DeRocco," he says, his voice rough like sandpaper. "*I'm* the shop owner. Now I'm going to ask you one final time, what brings you here?" I quake at the tone of his voice, my errand making me nervous as hell. One final time?

God I should've *known* he was the owner. Then why did the reviews online mention years of experience?

"I... I need some work done on a car," I stammer.

"It's...very important I get this work done, discreetly and promptly."

He quirks a brow, frowning.

"Discreetly?" he barks out.

I jump, then nod dumbly.

I squirm uncomfortably under his glare. I'm not used to being scrutinized like this, and I want to leave. It was a mistake giving him a fake name. He saw right through me.

"Your car?" he asks.

Shit. I need to get this over with and get the hell out of here. "No, actually," I say. "My...father's." I'm stammering like a bumbling teenager. "I was out with my...boyfriend, um, *ex*-boyfriend," I amend, because I *so* dumped his ass, "and we had a bit of an accident. The car is in a garage and needs to be towed.

"Let me get this straight," he says, in a voice that's almost like some kind of animalistic growl. If lions talked, they would sound like *this*. God, I was stupid. This guy definitely was the grumpy owner all the reviews talk about, and here I was thinking he maybe was friendly. "It's your *father's* car. Your boyfriend totaled it. And you're in here...why?"

"To have it *fixed* before my father gets back," I explain. It's a lot to explain, and do I even need to? "Listen," I say, my temper rising. "Can you just tell me already if you can fix it? I don't want to get into a lot of explanations and stuff. If you can't do the job, I need to find someone else."

A corner of his lips tips up. "Someone else? What kinda car is it?"

My stomach clenches. I practically whisper, "It's a 1967 Chevrolet Corvette Convertible."

He swears. "An L88?"

I whimper. "Yes."

"Honey," he says with a patronizing smile, "the next

mechanic that knows the ins and outs of a 67 Chevy Corvette is 300 miles from here and booked solid until January. That car's worth a cool two mil. You know that?"

My heart sinks. Is he joking? But no. Reviews online say this shop is worth dealing with the owner, because he knows his shit and he's literally *the only* one around here who does. I take in a deep breath and let it out again. "So you'll do it?"

The smile leaves his eyes. "I didn't say that." He leans over the counter. "First, tell me what the damage is."

With trembling hands, I take out my phone and pull up the pictures. He lets out a low whistle that tatters my already-frayed nerves. I want to cry. Instead, I stifle a whimper.

The rearview mirror is smashed, the windshield cracked right down the center, and the passenger door is bent beyond recognition. The bumper dangles crazily like a maniacal loose tooth.

He runs rough fingers over his beard and pulls, then his glacial stare swings back to me. "How the *fuck* did you do this to such a beautiful car?"

"I didn't do it," I snap. Didn't he listen at all? "My stupid boyfriend— *ex* boyfriend did it."

He shakes his head. "You were with him, you let him use the car, this is on *you*, babe." I blink. He might be the one with the power here, and I'm definitely screwed, but is it cool to call a potential customer *babe?*

He carries on. "And where's this ex now?" he asks. "Hope you dumped his ass. Jesus Christ, only dumb fuckin' morons damage a beauty like that."

I'm at my wit's end. I don't even *like* my ex anymore, but this guy's swift, and very clearly *crass* judgment, sets me off. No one talks to me this way. Hell, even my tutors and nannies have treated me with respect. Who the hell is this guy?

In my world, a bit of temper often gets you your way, so I haven't even tried to quell it. And I can't always help my temper. It might be a stupid move I'll regret, but it's too late.

I slam my hand down on the counter. "I'm not here to talk about my boy — *argh, ex*-boyfriend! I want to know, can you fix this car, how long it will take, and what you'll charge? *Please.*"

He places my phone down on the counter with slow, deliberate patience, his eyes on mine, and crosses those huge, scary arms over his muscled chest, fixing me with a stern glare that is completely unfamiliar to me. No one looks at Tanya Hayes that way. I swallow and take an involuntary step back from him.

He turns away from the desk and without a word, walks over to the shop door and flips a deadbolt into place.

Click.

Still without speaking, he goes to the front door and flips a second deadbolt.

Click.

Then he takes the *Open* sign and switches it around to show *Closed*.

Oh God. What's he going to do? Is he going to hurt me? Who the hell is he? I reach for my cell phone and don't know I'm going to do with it, but my hands are trembling so it clatters to the floor. I cringe, bend down to get it, but Levi gets it before I do. Our hands touch, and a zing of electricity skirts up my arm. I blink in surprise, and for a moment I wonder if he's pocketing my phone so I can't call for help before he abducts me or something, but he gives me the phone and I stagger backward.

Scowling, he stalks over to the leather loveseat that sits

against one wall with a stack of magazines featuring classic cars on the coffee table in front, and crooks a finger at me. I blink. Without a word, he points to the seat next to him.

What choice do I have?

Groaning inwardly and shaking like a goddamned leaf, I go to him.

Chapter Two

Levi

WHAT I WOULDN'T GIVE to put this beautiful, spoiled, headstrong little girl right over my lap and teach her to watch that mouth of hers. She comes in here looking like she's ready to walk a fucking runway, bosses me around like I'm her fucking butler, and hopes her tits and ass will get my attention?

Welll... Not gonna lie and say they didn't. I'm a red-blooded male and she's beautiful.

The shop's been closed for half an hour, a fucking advantage I'll use to my favor, and now I need to know what princess needs.

Christ, she's sexy as all fuck, and she knows it. She's got this little black dress that looks like it was tattooed on her, full cleavage I wanna bury my face in, a curvy, lusciously spankable ass, and her goddamn *hair*. It goes all the way down to her ass in thick waves, light brown with blonde and darker brown woven in. Her dark eyes are framed with thick, black lashes and brows, and she pouts when she looks at me with her full, beautiful lips. I want to take those lips between my teeth and feel her moan beneath me. My cock stirs to life. I shift on the loveseat.

I only just met her and there's one thing I know beyond a shadow of a doubt. No one's ever told this chick no in her life. I'd bet my ass no one's ever taken her in hand, either.

Maybe it's time someone did.

She walks over to me and eyes me with reservation, clutching her little purse against her side like I'm going to lift her wallet. Yeahhh. I'm *done* with this shit.

"Shop's closed, princess. You're on my personal time clock now. You want to talk details, sit your ass down."

"The shop's closed?" she says, her face falling and her lower lip jutting out a bit. I roll my eyes. This is a girl that is used to getting her way. She slumps onto the loveseat and sighs.

"Yeah," I say. What did she think, I was going to fix her car tonight? "So, deal is, I'm not fixing anything until I know exactly what I'm dealing with."

And who I'm dealing with.

"Spill. First, you tell me your real name and none of this Felicia shit. I won't even begin to discuss potential repairs until you do."

She frowns. "How'd you know that wasn't my real name?"

I just raise a brow at her. Does she think I'm a dumbass? Not even worth answering. I wait patiently.

"Fine," she says. "My father went on a business trip. He has half a dozen of these old-fashioned cars at home. Like a gallery," she says.

Half a dozen? So the princess comes from money. Noted.

"He doesn't drive them, like, *ever,*" she continues.

Understandable. "Smart," I grunt.

"I was visiting my parents, and Leon asked if we could take one of the cars out for a spin, since my dad wasn't home."

Seriously? What the hell is this shit? I glare at her. "What are you, seventeen?"

God, I hope not.

Her eyes flash at me, and her cheeks redden. "For your *information,* I'm twenty-seven," she snaps.

"And still sneaking out before curfew?" She really *does* need that pert little ass spanked.

She gets to her feet. "You know what, Mr. DeRocco? I didn't come here to be insulted." She tosses her head in the air and makes like she's leaving, but it's a bluff. She has no choice.

"*Sit,*" I half-growl. This girl is pushing her damn luck.

She glares at me, looks at the door, then bites her lip and flounces back on the loveseat. She knows she's screwed. And it *was* sort of a dickhead thing to say. Still, she needs to grow the fuck up.

"Continue," I order, folding my arms on my chest and watching her.

She takes in a deep breath, then lets it out slowly. "So I told him not to take the car out, and he found the key anyway. It was the easiest car to get out, since it's at the very front of the row of cars, and before I knew what was happening…" she cringes and buries her head in her hands.

"Dumbass *ex* crashes the car." I shake my head. "And he couldn't man the fuck up and get it repaired himself *why?*"

She shakes her head. "I don't know," she squeaks from behind her hands.

"Because he's a fuckin' douchebag, that's why," I supply for her.

She peeks out from around her hands. "You curse a lot," she notes.

I feel my brows shoot up. I cross my arms on my chest and give her a withering look. "Need to wash my mouth out with soap?"

Her cheeks flush a beautiful shade of pink. The shade of pink I'd see paint her chest when I made her come. The same color I'd turn her little ass over my knee.

I've got a pile of work that needs to be done before the next show and taking this work on will mean late nights. "And now you need this shit sorted before daddy gets home?"

She takes her hands away from her face and nods, her eyes pleading with me. And damn it if it doesn't make me want to help her. I can't say no. I must have some kinda fucking damsel in distress complex. A girl looks at me like that, and I have to say yes.

She opens her bag and pulls out three gold credit cards. "I have the money," she says. "Whatever you charge. I can even get you cash if you need it, just please, help me."

I frown at the cards. And then I read the emblazoned name on the front.

Tanya Hayes.

No. Fucking. Way.

She's heir to fucking *royalty*.

I take in a deep breath and stare at her. "Give me your real name, Felicia," I say, keeping my voice steady with effort. I want to hear her confirm that she really *is* Tanya Hayes, daughter of millionaire and Manhattan's classic car tycoon Reginald Hayes.

And she wants *me* to fix his goddamned car? I'm practically ready to have her sign a non-disclosure agreement. If

Hayes ever gets wind I laid a finger on his car… my mind wanders when I look her over.

Not sure which would make him blow a gasket sooner, touching his car or his daughter.

She swallows. "Tanya Hayes," she says, meeting my eyes, but wincing. She must see recognition written across my features. God.

"I know your father," I mutter.

"Of course you do," she groans. "Everyone does. But God, I can't let him know I came to you. *Please.*"

I look away and think over my options. Hayes is a competitor, and he's got fucking millions. He's got a reputation of getting whatever the fuck he wants whenever the fuck he wants it. He's ruthless and greedy, and I want nothing to do with him.

Where else is she gonna go, though? There *are* no classic car repair shops anywhere near here.

I don't want her money, though.

What the fuck am I doing? But I know I'm gonna go ahead with it anyway. And I'm a sick fucking bastard, so I don't want her money. She'll pay in other ways.

"Alright," I agree. "Let's talk over how I can help."

On impulse, she squeals and throws her arms around my neck. Jesus *Christ*. She smells so damn good she sends a bolt of electricity straight through me. What the hell is this? She's fucking electric. She's small and vulnerable in my arms and her skin feels like satin, silky and smooth. I pull away because my dick's starting to get ideas.

"Alright," I say, pulling her arms off me with difficulty and holding by the forearms so she's got to look up at me. I give her the sternest look I can. "But I don't want your money."

I'm such a fucking dick.

Her face falls, and she swallows. "What do you want?"

she asks, and I know she's thinking sex because there's betrayal in her eyes. But no.

She won't have to whore herself to me.

It's much better if she wants this.

"I need office help," I tell her, like I'm not totally planning on corrupting her. "I can't take money from Hayes in good conscience."

She frowns and tries to tug her arms away, but I hold fast. "It isn't my father's money. It's *my* money," she says with a glare. "Money I earned myself."

"Either way, I'm not touching Hayes money."

"Then what do you want?" she asks in a little voice, and for a second I feel bad for the girl. It can't be easy coming in here like this, all nervous as shit and wondering if some guy's gonna take advantage of you.

When I let go of her, she keeps her arms suspended in mid-air as if frozen.

"You work for me. Someone needs to tidy this damn place up, answer calls, and keep people happy. I'm doing good business because I'm the only one who offers this work for miles, but the place needs…a feminine touch."

Her eyes narrow. "How long do I work for you?"

"Well, let's see," I say. I get up, walk to the desk, and pull over the large calculator I keep there. "Work costs about this much," I say, punching in an estimate. "Let's say if you work… hmmm…" I factor some numbers in and look at the results. "Two weeks, full time, should do it."

Her jaw drops. "Two weeks?" she asks.

"Yep. Take it or leave it. You got any other work?"

Her cheeks flush. "Well, yeah, I do," she says, not meeting my eyes. "But it's flexible work, and I can do it anytime I want to." I want to know what that flexible work is she does, and why it makes her blush. I'll get it from her.

"Alright. You start tomorrow. Be here at 7 a.m. sharp.

People who work for me are treated well, but I expect you to be here on time and to do your work. Got it?"

"Yes, of course," she says, getting to her feet and looking around the shop. "Just…show up here at seven?"

I nod. "On the dot."

She smiles. "Yes, sir. Done."

Sir.

Yeah. I like that.

"Just so you know, I have rules for my employees." I let her feel the impact of my sharpened tone. I want her to hear this loud and clear.

"*Especially* for you." I smile at her. "We'll go over that tomorrow."

She nods tentatively. "Tomorrow," she repeats.

She'll see exactly what I have in mind.

Chapter Three

Tanya

THIS MAY BE the biggest mistake of my damn life. What am I *thinking?* At the first possible opportunity, I'm going to *kill* Leon. *Kill* him dead. Deader than dead. Maybe I can afford a hitman or something.

God. I can afford to have my ex-boyfriend murdered, but I can't use my money to fix the car? What kind of cruel joke is this?

I look over my wardrobe. What does one wear to a dirty auto body shop? Jeans and a t-shirt? Yeah, hell no. I want to look good for Levi. I finally settle on a plum-colored mini skirt and a cream-colored peplum top, the little Gucci handbag I bought in Italy, and a pair of spiky purple platforms. My calves look damn good in high heels, and I can't imagine I'll be on my feet for that long. I'll probably be answering phones and stuff all day.

I get to the shop at 6:55 on the nose, Starbucks venti

with skim milk in hand. No time for breakfast, though, but coffee is a must. The window into the shop looks dark, as if no one else is there yet, but he told me to be here at seven, so here I am.

I get out of my car, slide my phone into my purse, adjust the strap of my purse over my shoulder, and head to the entrance. I try the door, but it's locked. I knock, and ring a little bell next to it, but no response. I glance at my phone. It's now exactly seven on the nose.

Just when I'm about to head back to my car, I hear a rumble in the parking lot, and turn to see Levi pulling in in the most beautiful pale blue vintage car I've ever laid eyes on. I'm guessing this isn't one he drives regularly, and it's one he's brought in to work on, because it's chugging thick smoke from the exhaust and he drives it gingerly. But God, it's beautiful, all shiny and chrome, and the smell of diesel fills the air. I wave and he gives me a chin lift, then comes out of this car to meet me.

"Nice to see you're prompt," he says, as he takes out a large keychain. He unlocks the door and holds it open for me.

I enter the shop, and he flicks on the lights. "Today, I'll have you start with some dusting and window cleaning," he explains, snapping open shades and turning on lights. "But first, make us some coffee and take down the messages that were left overnight."

Wait a minute. Window cleaning? Dusting?

"Make us some coffee?"

"You want me to clean?" I ask, staring with chagrin at my beautiful outfit. His eyes look down my body appreciatively. A responding warmth hits my belly and my cheeks flush when his gaze rakes over me like he likes what he sees. He swallows.

Jacked Up

"Yeah. I said that yesterday, remember? Not sure you're dressed for the occasion, princess."

"Didn't know there was a dress code," I mutter, bristling at the damn *princess*.

Frowning, he goes under the desk and pulls out a ratty roll of paper towels that's somewhat discolored, and a huge bottle of glass cleaner that looks like it's been here for about twenty years.

"This will be a good start," he says. He hands me the bottle, gives one passing glance at my cleavage, then leaves and enters the shop. I sigh, my stomach rolling with hunger. I should've gotten the damn scone.

I spend a full hour cleaning the display cases. They're encased in dust, and it's no easy job to remove everything before I clean it. I make a note to myself to get some fresh paper towels and frickin *gloves*. My poor hands are red and chafed from the abrasive cleaner.

The door swings open with a jingle, and a guy I haven't met yet comes in. He whistles a cat call, and I bristle. The scent of cigars meets my nose and I wrinkle it in disgust. *Yuck.*

What the hell?

"Well helllooo," he says.

I smile through gritted teeth.

"Hello."

"And what have we here?" he asks, waggling his eyebrows. He's shorter than Levi and slighter, with a shaved head and neatly-trimmed goatee. He's got the *Jacked Up* logo on his jacket, and the name *Spade* emblazoned on the front. Gah-Reat. He works here?

I place the window cleaner down and extend my hand. "Tanya," I tell him. After Levi's reaction, I don't want him knowing who I am but I don't want to work a fake name here either.

He takes my hand and kisses the back. "Pleasure to meet you, Tanya," he says. I yank my hand away, creeped out. He makes my skin crawl and I'm not sure why, but I don't really care. There's nothing in my job description about this.

"Yeah, me too," I say, and turn my back to him. I continue cleaning, but he hasn't left me alone.

"And what brings you here?" he asks.

"Levi hired me," I respond shortly, cleaning away. The way he looks at me makes the little hairs on the back of my neck stand on end. My stomach rolls, and I'm not sure it's from hunger this time.

"Did he now? You know, you look really familiar."

God. What a classic pick-up line.

"Mmm," I say. "Not sure why." I flash him a plasticized grin and shrug my shoulders. "First office job. Now if you'll excuse me, I have work to do."

The door to the shop jangles and Levi enters the room. For some weird reason, my belly swoops and I feel a clear sense of relief. I hardly know the guy, but he's safer than this creep.

"Spade, did you meet our new hiree?"

"Yes, sir, I sure did," Spade says. "Was just thinking about asking her out for a drink when she told me she works here. We still have that no-dating company policy?" he asks with a chuckle.

Levi surprises me with his response. "We sure as fuck *do,*" he says, shooting me an angry glare. What the hell is that about? Like I asked this dipshit to hit on me? He should be glaring at the loser guy.

"Seriously?" Spade asks, the humor gone from his face.

Levi just shoots him a level glare, which pleases me because at least Levi is an equal opportunity glarer. "Yep. I want you to go take a look at that paint job on the '66

Ferrari and get started on it. It'll take a while, and I promised to have it back in record time."

"Shouldn't rush a paint job," Spade says with a frown.

Levi frowns back. "I'm asking you to do your job, and I cleared everything else off your schedule. You clock in, do your job, and let me worry about how long it takes to do it. " He jerks his chin at the door, dismissing the douchebag. "Now go."

Oddly, that gives me a little bit of a tingle. He's so damn bossy, and him telling other people what to do is weirdly hot.

Mumbling to himself, Spade takes his leave. I sigh audibly, but then draw in a breath and face Levi.

"All your employees so pleasant?" I ask, as I pull out coffee and stare at the machine. I've never seen anything like this in my life. We have the little pod coffeemaker things, and this is some sorta old fashioned coffee pot. Maybe even vintage. There's a pot and a button you push to turn it on, a reservoir for water, and a little plastic basket thing. I look sideways at Levi, hoping he can't see I don't know what the hell I'm doing.

I open the lid and pick up the can of coffee. I peel back the top. The aroma fills the room and my stomach rumbles again. I take the scoop and level it out, then lean over the pot. I have some sort of basic idea that I'm supposed to dump the coffee in this part so the water goes through it...I think. I'd google it but Levi is here, and he's watching me.

"So," I say, trying to make small talk. "How many people do you have working for you?"

"Twenty-five total," he says. "Though some are my West Coast connections that deal with shipping things across the country, and a few are my sales and marketing team."

I look at him in surprise. "You have a sales and

marketing team?" I expected him to say he had, like, four other guys here.

He shrugs and a corner of his lip quirks up. "Yeah."

Wow. I'm not sure why, but that impresses me. Just before I dump the grounds in the little plastic thing, he stops me with a loud, "*Stop.*"

I jump. I turn to him wide-eyed, still holding the coffee scoop in my hand. "What the hell?"

He's frowning at me, and he points to the coffee pot. "You have any idea how the fuck to make coffee?"

I worry my lip. "Well. Not really, no," I admit, looking away. I can't bear to see scorn in his eyes. It's so embarrassing.

"You have to put a filter in there, or you're gonna make a huge mess." He breathes in as if he's trying to be patient, then opens a cabinet above the coffee maker and takes out a white thing with frilled edges. He leans over me, his arm brushing mine, and a little shiver thrills through me. God, apparently I have some kinda badass blue collar fantasy or something, because just being near him's got my nerves zinging. I swallow, trying not to wobble on my heels, and watch what he does. He takes the paper thing and shoves it into the top of the coffee pot. He smells surprisingly good, strong and masculine and clean.

"Filter here," he growls. Then he takes out a spoon from a little drawer and begins measuring coffee. "Like this." He reaches across me again, his arm brushing mine, shuts the lid and hits an *on* button. The coffee pot starts sizzling and gurgling. I smile, as if I actually had something to do with it.

"Thank you," I say. He steps away, and my heart sinks. I like him close to me. He's so damn different from the other guys I've known. But he's my boss now, and I need to keep it together.

Jacked Up

He nods, but he's still frowning. The man frowns more than he smiles. I make it my mission in life to get him to smile more and not be so damn grumpy.

"You know," I say, eyeing him. "You want to improve your ratings in the shop, you might want to smile more. It'd be a good start." His frown deepens and his eyes cloud over, and suddenly I'm not so sure that was a smart thing to say. Definitely not safe. Being around Levi is dangerous.

The door to the shop dings and a beautiful blonde woman walks in. She's wearing designer jeans and a fitted t-shirt, and a pair of sunglasses she pushes on top of her head.

"Hi, Levi," she says, fluttering her manicured nails at him. The door to the shop shuts, and the peppery, floral smell of *Caron Poivre* fills the small interior. I know that perfume well. My younger sister begged for it for Christmas one year, and it reeked up her room like a French whorehouse. It cost like $500 a squirt.

I pretend to be tidying things behind the desk, but I'm really watching their interaction.

"Mandy," Levi says with a jerk of his head. She smiles at him, but he doesn't return the smile. He smiles at, like, no one, so this isn't impressive, but it makes me happy.

It surprises me that I care. Why the hell do I care?

They have a hushed conversation, and I try to ignore it, but can't help but notice how she jerks her head at me. I catch the word "help," and my cheeks flame. To say this job is beneath me is an understatement. He says a few things in a low voice I can't hear. By the time Barbie leaves the shop, I've managed to convince myself he's mocking me, and not only that? It's the only reason he hired me to begin with. To mock me, so he could poke fun at the spoiled Hayes princess.

It was a mistake coming here. I have no idea what else I'll do, but I need to figure it out.

"Okay," Levi says, standing behind the desk. "Slow day today and I've got two men working on projects now, so that gives us some time to go over the phones."

"Fine. Whatever." I don't like the way he gossiped about me with the blonde, so I don't see any real need to be polite. At least that's what I think, until one of his dark eyebrows shoots up and he fixes me with that stern glare that disintegrates my panties.

"Excuse me?" he asks, in a low growl that makes my belly clench.

"I said *fine,*" I repeat, but less terse this time. I'm irritated that he's making me waste my breath like this. "Let's do it."

He gives me another look, then shakes his head and points to the phones. He picks it up and shows me how to hold and transfer calls.

"Perfect," I mutter, wondering how I'm going to disinfect the phone every time I need to use it. I may need gloves or something. I stand in front of the phone like a soldier prepared for battle. I came, I saw, I will conquer. To my surprise, he's behind me now, trying to show me what to do on the phone, but he's effectively caging me in against the desk. I shiver.

"Think you've got it?" he asks.

I'm starving and grumpy and my feet hurt, so I snap. "Whatever. You can go back to the shop now."

His heat warms my back, and he's way too damn close. His voice comes up to my ear, rough and raspy and stern as fuck. "Not a fan of your tone of voice right now, little girl," he says in my ear.

For some reason, that makes my body do strange, terrible things.

No one's ever called me *little girl* before. I'm suddenly vulnerable, and I don't like it.

"I don't know what you're fucking talking about," I snap. I turn to him but blink in surprise when I realize how close he is, so close his breath makes the tendrils of hair on my forehead skitter across my skin.

"Yeah, you do," he says, in a knowing rumble. "So you watch that tone of voice."

I try to frown at him, but my glare is like a little matchstick trying to stand up to a roaring fire. When he scowls, and I take an involuntary step back.

"I told you yesterday my employees have rules," he grits out. "The first I have for *you* is no backtalk." He reaches over, and to my shock, tugs a strand of my hair.

"Ow!"

"The second rule, you do nothing stupid and dangerous."

"What?"

He shakes his head and I swallow.

"Third," he plows on, "and this is important, so pay attention." His voice lowers and deepens. "Only mechanics enter the shop."

I nod dumbly.

"Catching on?"

"Yep."

"You're a smart girl."

I nod and huff out a breath. "Yeah. Okay. Yes, *sir*." I try to make it sound mocking, but it doesn't quite work.

What does he do if I break those rules? Fire me? Something tells me it's worse than that.

He points to the desk and for one crazy minute I expect him to tell me to bend over it, like he wants to spank me or fuck me or maybe both and hell if the idea doesn't make my hands shake.

"Pick up the phone, Tanya," he whispers in my ear.

I do what he says, my hands shaking.

"Good girl." He reaches around me, his heat surrounding me like a circle of fire. I look at his tats. Even his fingers are tattooed, all up and down the front and sides.

"God, did it hurt?" I ask.

"What?" he asks.

"Those hand tats."

He huffs out a breath, almost like a laugh but not quite. "Yeah, babe. Tattoos hurt." Then he shrugs and his voice drops. "But sometimes, even things that hurt feel good."

What the hell is he talking about? Damn it, I wanna know. I want him to hurt me good.

Wait, *what*? Who the hell am I?

He shows me a whole bunch of things and even though it makes sense, I'm not sure I'm not gonna fuck this up when it's time.

"When I'm in the shop you take a message. Unless it's a life or death emergency, I'll return the calls on lunch."

"Got it, boss," I say, wiping a hand across my brow. I give him a salute as he prepares to head back in the shop.

As soon as the door clangs shut behind him, the phone rings. I turn and look at it as if it's the command center for NASA. What was I supposed to do again?

Biting my lip, I pick up the receiving. "Hello, Jacked Up Mechanics. How can I help you?"

I hear a dial tone. *Shit*. I did something wrong. I push another button, and another, and now the display's lit up like a Christmas tree. I feel stupid. Tears blur my vision. I swallow and read the numbers on the dial, hang up the phone, and stare. Finally, with a deep breath, I lift the receiver again and hit the blinking button that says "1." I figure it's a good start.

Jacked Up

Someone starts talking to me and I huff out a sigh of relief. I take down the information, and promise Levi will call them back, then hang that one up and go to the second call. This one, however, is more insistent.

"Put Levi on the phone," a deep voice grits out.

"I'm sorry, he's in the shop right now, but I will take a—"

"I don't give a shit what he's doing, I said put him on the goddamned phone."

"That isn't possible, sir," I say through gritted teeth. The next thing I know the man is screaming so loudly at me I have to hold the receiver away from my ear. He says horrible, nasty things and makes me feel like I'm about two.

Will telling him off get me fired? I have no idea how to handle this so I put the call on hold and turn to the shop. I push the door open, and almost collide into Spade. "You're not supposed to be in here," he mutters. "Levi catches you in here, your ass is grass."

His eyes predictably travel to my ass. I glare at him and push past, looking for Levi.

There are people all around me working, under the hoods of cars, one man spray-painting something in the back, another working with wires. All eyes come to me and work momentarily freezes. Shit. This was not a good move. I swallow, ignoring the unwanted attention.

"Where's Levi?" I ask in my bravest voice.

A hush goes over the shop when I hear Levi's voice right in my ear.

"What the hell did I tell you about coming into this shop?"

His hand's on my elbow. To my chagrin, he's marching me back into the office like a child being escorted to the principal's office. When we get to the entrance the noise in the shop resumes but Levi yells over his shoulder, "Lunch break. Go!"

Tools clang and voices shout at one another.

He pushes open the door to the office, drags me in, and slams the door behind him. "I gave you three—" he begins but I interrupt him.

"Phone call," I say, yanking my arm out of his grip. "And I'll have you know that man on the line screamed at me and berated me and called me all sorts of names because I told him you couldn't talk to him right away."

He quirks a brow. "That right? So you decided the response was to cave and give him what he wanted?" he asks. His voice is practically a growl, so laced with heated anger I feel my cheeks warm.

I nod and shrug at the same time. I'm embarrassed I did this, so I try to cover my embarrassment with indignation. Maybe it'll distract him.

"Maybe I did," I huff out.

"Not sure it was the smartest move," he says, jaw clenched. "Someone acts the part of an asshole, the last thing I do is give them what they fuckin' want."

Noted. Damn it.

"Well maybe I didn't ask you," I snap. I look away. I'm embarrassed and I don't want him to know.

He lifts the receiver and points a finger at me, ordering me to stay put.

Fuck. He isn't done with me yet. What'll he do?

I look wildly around the shop for some sort of escape, but all I see is that coffee's finally made, and the men have all taken off for lunch. The shop is empty.

I walk over to pour myself a cup of coffee when Levi answers the phone.

"Levi DeRocco." A few seconds later, he barks out a stern, "*Enough.*"

Jacked Up

He pauses. I'm trying to dump little packets of half and half in my coffee but the tone of his voice catches my attention. I drop the little half and half and it splatters on the counter.

"You do not call my office and speak to my staff the way you did," he grits into the phone. "Raise your voice one more time, and you can come pick up your half-finished car and pay the remainder of the invoice owed. You can tow that car to another shop that'll put up with your shit because this ain't one of 'em."

He listens, his eyes still fixed on me. "You'll apologize to my desk help when you come here on Friday, and you'll watch your tongue," he continues. I blink in surprise. He really doesn't take shit from anyone. "Now are you gonna speak like an adult, or do we need to end this conversation?"

He pauses, listening. "Yes, sounds good. I was clear as hell when I'd have this work done for you, and it ain't my fault your showman's decided to take you touring early. Now I'll see what I can do to accommodate you, but I want to be sure we're clear that bullying my staff isn't how we'll handle things like this going forward."

He says a few more things, but I'm intent on sipping the coffee. It's surprisingly good and takes away a little of my hunger. Maybe I've had too much coffee, though, because when he drops the receiver, I jump.

"Now," Levi says in a low, controlled voice. "I deal with you. Tanya."

I look up at him sheepishly. He's standing against the wall with his arms crossed on his chest. "Three little rules," he says, shaking his head. He lifts one tattooed, enormous hand, and crooks a finger at me. "C'mere."

"I think I'm okay, actually," I stammer. "I haven't eaten

all day, and I'm starving. I was thinking maybe I'd go and take my lunch break—"

"Come. *Here.*"

So apparently I have no choice. I walk over to him so that we're a few feet apart and stare at him. I screwed up with the rules, and I'm about to find out what that means in Levi's shop.

Chapter Four

Levi

I'm about to fuck up the rules of office etiquette so goddamned bad there will be no going back. But damn it, I mean what I say and every motherfucker who walks through the doors to this shop knows that. Even the damn customers.

Apparently, it's time Tanya learned that.

And if I'm honest? I didn't hire the girl for her secretarial skills.

I was maybe hoping she'd fuck up and give me a reason to punish her.

She stands in front of me now, a good head shorter than I am even with those death-defying fuck-me heels on. Her top's tucked neatly into her skirt, and she stands erect, but there's a smudge on her white top and a smear across the top of her nose. We'll have a talk about appropriate office attire later. But first, we'll talk about rules.

"Three rules," I say, fixing her with a stern glare. "No backtalk. Nothing stupid and dangerous. And you do not enter the shop. Did you break any of my rules?"

She bites her lip and nods. "Well…yeah," she says, looking away. I reach for her chin and bring her gaze to mine. Her lips part and her eyes are half lidded. She's supposed to be chastened, but instead she looks like she's ready for me to yank that skirt up and fuck her up against the desk.

I need to touch her. It breaks every rule there is about office protocol and shit, but who am I kidding? I didn't hire her because I'm a fucking professional.

I want to touch her long, gorgeous, chestnut-colored hair. Instead of weaving my fingers through it and giving her the good, hard pull she needs, I tuck one stray lock behind her ear, barely touching her. We're so close I can hear the steady tempo of her heartbeat. Her eyes widen when I tuck the hair, her lips parting. My dick tightens against my pants because I know exactly what needs to happen next.

"You fucked up, Princess," I whisper in her ear. "Turn around, and bend over that desk."

I expect a little tirade. Outrage. Huffing and puffing and indignation. But she closes her eyes briefly, as if to steel herself, and to my surprise, she doesn't protest. When she opens her eyes they're fixed on me and heated. She licks her lips.

She wants this as much as I do.

With torturously slow movements, she circles around and puts her back to me, then leans over so deliberately it's slow motion, her belly hitting the desktop, fingers spread wide to hold herself in place. Her ass is on full display, voluptuous and full and in such fucking desperate need of a spanking.

I lean over, letting my flank press up against her back. "Your daddy ever spank you, Tanya?"

Jacked Up

She shakes her head from side to side, her breath a husky whisper.

I place my hand on her lower back. The guys won't be long on break, and this needs to happen.

"One thing you'll learn, princess," I say, resting my hand on the swell of her ass, which breaks every rule in the office handbook but I don't give a shit, "is that *this* daddy won't hesitate."

She releases a strangled cry, and I haven't even spanked her yet. She's wet for me. I can tell by the way she trembles and breathes heavily she's turned on. If I lifted her skirt and pulled away that little strip of fabric over her pussy, she'd coat my hand with her arousal. Tanya likes being dominated.

Fucking.

Noted.

Without another word, I raise my hand and slam it against the underside of her ass. She raises up on her toes and lets out a little yelp. Her knuckles whiten on the desk, but she stays there belly-down. Maybe she knows she can't get away.

Maybe she wants more.

I lift my hand and slap my palm against her ass a second time, a third, and a fourth, each stinging swat landing in a different place. My palm tingles from where it connects with her ass, and my dick lengthens. "You stay the fuck out of that shop," I growl, spanking her again, and again, "or the next time you do, I'll bare your ass before I spank it."

And I fucking will. The thought of spanking her bare ass makes my dick painfully hard, but I'm not fucking around here. Yeah, I want to fuck the princess heiress and hard, but I'm not screwing around when it come to safety.

"You'll watch your tone of voice," I say with another sharp spank. "And stay the fuck out of that shop. It's dangerous in there." I spank her three more times in rapid succession. "And the truth is, I'll fucking kill someone if they so much as look at you." She whimpers. I can feel the heat on her ass straight through that little skirt of hers. She's had enough for now.

I mean every word I said but I think my point's been made. I want to heave up this skirt and rake my hand up along her inner thighs, then finger her until she soars into her climax. I bet she's damp with need and her skin feels like silk. I'd bet a goddamn mint she tastes sweet, too. I make it my aim to find out.

But not now. Not yet.

I right her skirt, and pull her to standing, then spin her around to look at me. Taking her by the chin, I bring her eyes to mine. "You hear me?"

Her wide, bright eyes blink up at me. Then she lashes flutter again, as if waking from a trance. She swallows. "Did you just spank me?" she whispers.

I huff out a laugh. "No, babe. I just gave you a motivational massage." She blinks and stares, as if she doesn't know what to do with herself. I hear the guys entering the shop behind me, tools being lifted and voices in the background. I gotta go.

"You just spanked me," she repeats. It's like she's still trying to process what just happened.

I raise a brow to her. "Your point?"

"You shouldn't do that," she whispers.

I lean in and whisper in her ear. "You mean to tell me you didn't like it?"

She swallows. "No, Levi," she whispers back, her fingers gently grasping my shoulder. "Problem is, I liked it way too fucking much."

Footsteps sound right outside the door and we pull

away just in time, but I'm sure we look like teens caught making out in a school parking lot, because Spade freezes when he comes into the shop.

"Boss, need some help with the finish," he says. He pulls a cigar butt out of his mouth. Son of a bitch knows there's no smoking in the shop. If this guy wasn't so fucking good at what he did, I'd fire his ass, but he does better detail work than anyone on the East Coast.

"You smoking in the shop?" I ask him.

"Nah," he says. He gives Tanya a lewd grin. "Leftover butt from lunch. Was just chewing on it."

She wrinkles up her nose in disgust. I don't like how he looked at her.

"Show me what you need," I say, pushing open the door to the shop.

When the door shuts, he looks over his shoulder at me. "You banging the office help, boss?" he asks. "Getting a little protective there."

I could slug him. Hell, my hand tingles just thinking about it. Instead, I force myself to exhale slowly so I don't snap. "Mind your own fucking business," I tell him. Who the hell does he think he is? "Did you somehow forget that you're working for me here?"

He grins. "Nah, boss. Believe me," he says, tapping his temple. "I remember everything."

Fucking certifiable. I ignore his idiotic rumblings and look at what he needs to show me. Nicked exterior. I finger the edge of the damage and give him my best advice. "Then finish it right to make sure it gleams. Get this done by five?"

He nods, wipes his hand on a rag, and picks up a tool.

"Sure thing." He winks, the butt still dangling from his lips. "Gonna get *her* done by five?"

Without thinking I grab him by the scruff of the neck

and haul his ass up so we're eyeball to eyeball. "Don't care that you're the best fucking detail man money can buy. You say one more word about Tanya and me, and your ass is on the street. Got it?" His eyes widen, then shutter. He holds his hands up in surrender.

"Okay, okay," he says, garnering the attention of several in the shop. "Just let me down!"

I drop him back and he stumbles into the car, then turn to face whoever else is watching, but they all slink away to their respective jobs. I never lay a hand on my employees. Today, I did it twice.

God, I need a drink.

I throw myself into my work and try not to think about the way her ass felt beneath my hand. Her half-lidded eyes, and what she said before I returned to the shop.

Problem is, I liked it way too fucking much.

It's a dare. A promise.

She's just thrown down that gauntlet.

We have two weeks.

One job.

Fuck etiquette.

Chapter Five

Tanya

I TRY hard to focus on the work I need to do, but it's practically hopeless. I've managed to get the whole phone thing down, but it seemed that slew of calls all at once was really the exception to the rule. The phone doesn't ring all that much the rest of the day, and the few calls that come in are locals with very minimal work that needs recording. I'm getting the hang of it but getting dizzy. There's a little room the size of a closet adjacent to the main sitting area, and I find a vending machine and soda. I gratefully grab a bag of peanut M&M's and reason they're protein, and wash it all down with a Diet Coke.

Doing this normal stuff isn't helping, though. Like, not even a little. I'm completely distracted, and it's all his fault.

I can hear the sounds of machines whirring and the guys shouting to each other in the shop, and every time I hear Levi's deep growl, my body teems with an electric vibe, like his voice is somehow connected to my pussy.

I can't believe he spanked me. And even more? I can't believe I *liked* it.

Holy hotness. Liked it? My panties are wet. Every time I move, I feel the way my skirt chafes against my stinging ass, and it reminds me what it was like to be pushed over that desk and punished by him. I can still feel his huge palm slam against my ass, still feel the pressure of his hand pushed into my lower back holding me in place, and my mind is racing with fantasies.

I want him to do it again.

He threatened to bare my ass if I went back into the shop. I eye the door with the fascination of a child. I've been told not to go in, so it's the only thing I can think about doing. I imagine what it would be like to encounter him all angry and furious. He'd wipe his hands, march me back into the office, push me over the desk and pull my panties down.

I close my eyes and can't breathe. Can't think.

The phone rings and I'm so grateful for something to do, I pick it up again.

I take down the information when I hear Levi come in the office. "Message for me?" he asks.

I nod, proud of myself that I actually handled the phone call well this time. "Dane Carter," I say. "Dane has a client in his construction company who's got a car that needs attention and was hoping you could give him a moment of your time. There was also a woman checking in on the status of her paint job, and an old man with a reedy voice named Barney who asked if you've found the spare to his key."

Levi nods and heads back to the shop when the phone rings again.

Only this time, I recognize the voice on the other end of the line.

Jacked Up

The M&M's and soda didn't help. I need something way stronger after this day.

I think the only way he hasn't suspected it's me is because first of all, I've said one word: "hello." And second of all, he isn't expecting me to answer *this* phone.

"Certainly, sir," I say in a high-pitched sing-song voice, and I add on some kinda European accent for good measure. "I vill tell our boss of your most urgent request. Please allow me to take down your information." I jot the number down, and when I hang up the phone I hear a snort of laughter. My cheeks flame.

I turn to see Levi leaning against the doorway. "What the hell was that?" he asks, eyeing me curiously. "Getting bored? Do I need to give you more work to do?"

I frown at him and lift my nose into the air. "That was my *father*," I say, making sure I glare sufficiently so he knows he should take me seriously. "I couldn't go on letting him hear me, so I had to…think quick. You should be impressed, you know," I say, huffing out a breath. "Instead of *mocking* me like…like…a big meanie."

He quirks an eyebrow up and I swear he's got like a magical line directly to my body, because even the littlest look of rebuke and I'm all hot and bothered. I turn away from him and go back to the desk, pretending I don't want him to kiss me. Or touch me. Or do dirty, wicked things with his mouth.

He's asking me something, but the blood's rushing so hard in my ears I don't hear him at first. I click the end on my pen and lean over to put it in the mug he's got on the desk, turning around to look at him. "What was—"

My pinky finger hooks the handle of the cup. The pens cascade to the floor, and the mug falls to the floor and shatters.

"Oh for *fuck's* sake," I curse, reaching for the broken pieces.

"Leave them," he growls. "Let me get the dustpan and broom."

"I'm fine," I protest, reaching for a large shard, but when I crouch down I wobble on my heel, my hand slips, and the broken glass slices into my finger. I yelp and pull away, crimson blood staining my finger. It fucking hurts. Levi curses under his breath, reaches for my hand, and grabs a box of tissues from the desk. He wraps a few around my finger and puts a little pressure.

"I told you not to touch that," he scolds, still holding my hand. "Don't you ever do what you're told? Goddamn it, should've spanked you harder."

"I'm a big girl," I protest. "Just slipped is all. Accidents happen."

"And a fuck of a lot more accidents happen when you do stupid shit like going into the shop when I tell you not to and reaching for the glass when I tell you *not to.*"

I yank my hand away from him. "Jesus, I'm fine," I mutter. "I can take care of myself."

He glares at me when the blood starts dripping down my finger again. "That remains to be seen. You, princess, likely need stitches."

It suddenly dawns on me that this could be a serious situation. Like…what if there's a scar or something?

I look down at the cut and shake my head. "I hate doctors. I'll take care of this on my own first and see what I can do."

Leaning back on his haunches, he fixes me with a stern stare. "How did you get here?" he asks. I can't believe this is the same guy that actually laughed a few minutes ago. Now he looks like he could freeze water into glaciers with a mere glance.

Jacked Up

"Drove," I mutter. I swallow hard. My finger's starting to throb. I need some pain relievers or something. My eyes water when I wrap the tissues around it again to stop the bleeding, but the tissue dampens in my hands and he has to hand me a stack of fresh ones.

"*I'm* driving you home," he says. "When we get there, we'll bandage your hand. And if it looks like you need stitches, I'll throw you over my goddamned shoulder and take you into the ER myself if I need to." He's all growly and angry, but there's a part of me that sorta likes it because my hand is throbbing and I don't really want to think about what to do right now. I'm retreating in my head like a child. It hurts and all I want to do is cry, but I'd be embarrassed if I did that, so instead I swallow real hard and just nod.

"Fine." I'm embarrassed and hungry and tired. I blink back tears as I get to my feet and follow him out of the shop.

"What'd your father want?" he asks. The door to the shop shuts. God, I forgot all about my father. What a mess I've walked into here. I'm such a *loser*.

"He has something he wants you to look at," I say. "I wrote it down on the desk. I'm sorry, I don't remember."

He leads me to one of the biggest trucks I've ever seen. I swear to God the tires are so big they're like up to my armpits. It's definitely not the pretty car he drove in this morning. Figures he has a lot of different wheels he drives though.

"What the hell is this thing?" I ask, standing back and staring in awe. I think if I squint my eyes, I can see it breathing like some kinda jungle beast, smoke coming out of the exhaust pipes and grate in front. "This looks like… one of those Monster Truck things. Do you ride this in those shows?"

He huffs out a laugh. "Yeah, no. This is just a truck, babe. Now get in." I amble awkwardly to the door, but before I can figure out how to haul my ass up and get onto this thing, I feel him grab me right under the armpits and hoist me straight up into the air so I can get my footing. I hold my injured hand in the air and gasp, then step into the cab of the truck and sink into the seat.

He joins me a minute later, gets into the driver's seat, and fires up the engine. When it roars to life, I feel the rumble beneath me. We're so high up here. On top of the world. I can see for miles. Regular cars look like mere toys, and even the local public transportation buses look tiny compared to this monster of a truck.

"Buckle your seatbelt," he orders.

"This is amazing," I say breathlessly, as he pulls into the street and I do what he says. The engine purrs now when he easily navigates it and out of the streets. The rich smell of the leather interior fills the cab, and the seat's warm beneath me. I don't know if it's because Levi's bossy and dominant and manhandles the hell out of me, or because I'm seriously sex-deprived and *need* to get some soon, but there's something about being in this truck that's making me all hot and bothered. This cab's fucking sexy. I look out the window, pretending his truck isn't turning me on. There's just something so raw and masculine about it. It's clean and bare inside here, and just warm enough I'm starting to feel comfortable.

"Where to, princess?" he asks.

I tell him my address. "I don't want to leave my car at the shop overnight," I tell him. Not only is it ridiculously expensive, but I don't want anyone at the shop seeing it in the morning and getting any ideas.

"You're not," Levi says, taking a left, then accelerating. "I'm having one of my men pick it up and bring it to your place later." He gives me a sidelong look. "How's that hand?"

A lump rises in my throat and I swallow. It hurts like fucking *hell* and I'm a little scared to look at it. I hate needles, and don't want to go to the doctor if I can help it.

"It's alright," I lie, but he's not stupid. A big, calloused hand reaches out and rests on my knee. He gives me a little squeeze when he chides me in his low, rough voice.

"Tell the truth, Tanya."

Tears spring to my eyes. "It hurts," I say in a little voice that sounds so childish to my own ears, my cheeks flame with embarrassment.

"I'm sure it does," he says gently. "I mean, how's the bleeding?"

Gingerly, I pull the tissues away and look with a grimace. "Well…I think it looks better," I mutter. "I mean it's still totally gross, but I don't think I need stitches."

He pats my knee in an almost-swat that's both affectionate and attention-grabbing. "Something tells me you'd say that if you were bleeding out."

I bite my lip. He's not wrong.

"Will it scar?" I ask. I grimace, thinking about the jobs I have lined up next week. I haven't said anything to him and won't. Not yet, when he has me working for him and I need the damn car fixed.

"If it needs stitches and you don't get them, sure as fuck might," he growls.

I worry my lip in silence.

"Why are you so worried about scarring?" he asks. "It won't be ugly if that's what you're worried about. It's on the inside of your hand and people will hardly see it."

"I just am," I say, not liking the way he's dismissing me like my concerns don't matter. My stomach rumbles with hunger, and my head feels a little lightheaded. I put my head back on the seat and close my eyes. He doesn't reply.

After a minute I need to open them again to tell him where to go, and soon we pull up outside of my apartment building.

"Thank you, Levi," I say. "I really appreciate you driving me. I can take it from here."

I know he has every intention of coming upstairs with me, and part of me wants that. But first, I'm not sure where the hell this beast of a truck would park, and second, his guy's dropping off my car and what if he sees Levi's truck here? Third…if I get alone with him, I'm not sure what will happen. I like to be in control when I'm alone with a guy, and with Levi, I'm anything but.

"Cute," Levi says. "Like I'm gonna drive you home and drop you off and trust that you'll take care of that fucking hand." He shakes his head, narrowing his eyes on the road. "Well lookie here. On-street parking until morning, and I don't need a resident pass for this side of the street." He looks at me and shoots me a half-smile. "Let's go upstairs."

Chapter Six

Levi

It comes as no surprise that the princess lives in the lap of fucking luxury. I lift her out of the truck, steady her on her feet, then take her uninjured hand and lead her to the main entrance. This place is huge, towering into the night like a castle. There must be several hundred apartments, complete with valets and door attendants. This place couldn't be more different than mine.

I smile to myself. And I've got her dirtying her hands in my shop for the next two weeks.

The doorman opens the door, and I'm not sure if he's more concerned with her hand or me. He eyes me with suspicion, then stares at her hand.

"Did you injure yourself, Ms. Hayes?" he asks, his eyes dark with concern. The door shuts and he stands dutifully in his navy uniform, staring at her hand, then me.

"Yeah," she says. "Just cut it on a piece of glass. I'm

fine though. My friend Levi was just helping me upstairs to bandage it up."

He raises a brow to me and I give him a look that says *Back off, motherfucker.* We're from different generations, different sides of the street, but we both speak the same language. He takes a physical step back and nods.

"Please ring if you need assistance, Ms. Hayes," he says, pushing the call button on the elevator and giving me a look like the assistance she might need is pulling me off her. Jesus.

"Thank you," she says. We step onto the elevator when the mirrored doors open. "Fourteenth floor," she says, jerking her chin at the floor numbers. There are twenty-five floors in this place. I hit the fourteen and watch as the gleaming doors glide shut. I barely restrain flipping off High and Mighty at the door. The interior is mirrored like the outside, and I take the opportunity to stare at her reflection. She's still beautiful as all hell, long legs and creamy skin, hair that hits just above her ass. In the mirror, her face is paler than it was today at the shop, and I wonder if it's because of her hand. I stand next to her still in my work clothes, thick beard, tats on every inch of exposed skin. We look so different it's almost amusing. No, it *is* amusing, like we were paired up on one of those damn reality shows or something.

We glide in silence upward. Just as the elevator cruises to a gentle stop, I ask myself what the fuck am I doing. I can't go swooping in to rescue every fucking damsel in distress. Especially not this one. She's been bred on caviar and champagne. If anything between us went wrong and her father caught wind of it, I'd be fucked. He's a man with power and influence.

Well, so am I.

But when the doors swing open and she steps out, I

reach for her elbow to steady her. My hand touches her creamy skin and she turns those large, wide eyes to me, and I forget Raymond Fucking Hayes.

The elevator opens up to a hall with a chandelier, large framed prints on the walls, and a plush burgundy carpet. We don't have a long hall to walk down to get to her apartment. This is the anteroom to her penthouse right here. She doesn't live on the fourteenth floor. She *owns* it.

She presses her thumb to a large panel outside the door, and a little green light flashes, I hear a faint pop, and she opens the door.

"Come in," she says, not meeting my eyes. Is she embarrassed?

I follow her in.

"This a three bedroom?" I ask curiously, leaning back against the wall and surveying it. Everything's modern and opulent, shiny and new.

She nods.

"What do you do with the other bedrooms?" I ask.

"Well, one's an office," she says. "And the other's for work."

"Yeah? What do you do for work?" I'm imagining she shuffles papers for her daddy and earns a cool mil. I busy myself at reading the wine labels she's got in the wine case built into the wall in her dining room, so she doesn't see the scorn on my face.

But she doesn't answer. She's checking her phone and not looking at me.

"Tanya?"

She looks over curiously.

"What do you do for work?"

"Oh," she says, looking away and not meeting my eyes. She's trying to evade me, and I'm not sure why. "I do lots of things."

Evasion isn't cool, but we'll deal with that later.

"Show me where your bathroom is. Do you have first aid supplies, or do we need to call the guy downstairs?"

"Well, I think I have what I need," she says. "But we'll see."

I follow her to the bathroom, and she points to the cabinet below the sink. When I open it, I see a vibrant red bag. "This?"

She nods, looking pale again, like she might faint.

"Go sit down," I order sternly, pointing to her bedroom. All I need is for her to topple over and whack her head or something.

She sits, holding her injured hand in front of her while I open the first aid kid and assess what's inside. I take out some materials and line them up on the counter. "Should have what we need here," I say to her. I walk into her room. It's dim in here, lit only by a closet light she left on. I flick the lamp on her bedside table so I can see what I'm doing better. "You'll have to let me take a look."

Fear flashes in her eyes, and she shakes her head from side to side. "I think it's okay," she says. "I can actually bandage it up myself now." She's sitting on the edge of the bed, but it's one of those high jobs with a slippery cover, so she's having to hold herself up by pushing her toes into the carpet. She reaches for the bandages. "I can do it," she insists.

Bullshit.

"Tanya," I say warningly, but she sets her jaw and her eyes go flinty. For fuck's sake. Yeah, I've got no patience for this shit.

"Give me your hand," I order.

She shakes her head from side to side.

So that's how we're gonna play it. I know she's just

freaked out, and some people act crazy when they're scared, but this isn't cool.

I lean in and take her chin between my thumb and forefinger, forcing her to maintain eye contact with me.

"Do you remember what happened to you in the shop today when you didn't do what you were told?"

She swallows and looks away but nods. She shifts a little on her seat.

I continue in a low, steady voice, so I don't freak her out but she understands my point. "You want that to happen again?"

She doesn't answer, and I stifle a chuckle. She does.

"The next time won't be the kind of spanking you like, little girl," I warn her, but the threat only seems to make her even more eager. She licks her lips. I remember her response in the office earlier, but at this point I'll use whatever tool I have to get her to cooperate.

"Now you do what daddy says and give me your hand, Tanya." I give her a stern, warning look. "*Now.*"

She bites her lip and offers me her hand, wincing when I remove the tissues.

"Good," I say gently, taking her hand in both of mine. "So let's get this cleaned up so I can get a better look, okay?"

She nods silently.

I find a washcloth in the bathroom, wet it in warm water, squeeze it out, then return to her and gently dab the wound. It's actually nowhere near as bad as I suspected, and after I clean it up, a few bandaids do the trick. Her hand shakes in mine when I place the last bandage in place.

We're so wrong for each other. I'll ruin her. Tear her pretty little clothes and mark that perfect skin. But I can't help myself. I've always wanted class. She's fucking perfection.

When she's good and cleaned up, I take her hand to my mouth and place a gentle kiss on top. She needs a gentle touch to come undone and fuck if I can't be the one to give it to her.

"Good girl," I say approvingly, watching as a small smile tugs at her lips. I like my women to submit to me, and I can't help but go all daddy on a girl like Tanya. I need to get to know her better, but if I have my way, that'll involve her legs wrapped around me while she screams *daddy*. I'm crouched in front of her, her legs are slightly apart, and my cock gets hard at the shadow between her knees.

"Thank you," she says in a husky whisper that makes my dick hard. She swallows and licks her lips. My mind goes to those gorgeous, slightly parted knees in front of me. All I'd have to do is spread those knees, hike that skirt up a little more…

Without a word I let my hand rest on her upper thigh. "Do you need something for the pain?" I ask, giving her a gentle squeeze. Her breath catches and she parts her knees just a little bit more.

"I'm good," she whispers.

I move my hand up higher, so that the knuckle on my middle finger grazes the hem of her skirt. I shake my head.

"You're not," I tell her, leaning in so my mouth is against her ear. "I should punish you for lying."

Her full breasts heave with the effort of breathing. "Maybe you should," she whispers.

With both hands on her thighs now, I let my thumbs roam higher, so close my hands are fully under her skirt. "I'll have to think about the best way to punish you," I say into her ear. "Should I take you across my knee?"

She moans.

"Maybe I should bring you to the edge of coming and leave you there, swollen and hot and ready to split wide open," I tease, taking her lobe between my teeth and gently biting.

Her breath gets all ragged.

"Maybe I'll clamp those nipples and leave you tied spread-eagled while I torture you?"

She whimpers.

"Or should I lay you over that bed and whip you with daddy's belt? Make you finger yourself and dream of daddy's fingers on that sweet little pussy? You'll have to earn those, baby, by being a good little slut for daddy."

She stops breathing then, like she's on the cusp or orgasm already and one breath of air will make her shatter.

"All of that," she whispers. "I...need to be punished with all of that."

Jesus fucking Christ. She's giving me the green light to fulfill whatever fucking fantasy I want. I thread my fingers through her long, thick, silky hair, and pull her head back.

"Let's start by taking those clothes off," I order. "Take off everything but your panties. *Those*, princess, are mine."

I release her and stand, crossing my arms on my chest so I can make sure she does what she's told. I'm not fucking around when I tell her what to do. I want to see my handprint on her ass when I fuck her, my teeth mark on her neck when she screams my name.

Her eyes on me, she lifts her top from the hem and slowly rakes it up over her skin, then stands and shimmies out of her skirt. Full, luscious breasts half-covered by a push-up black lace bra. Lightly tanned, silky skin just waiting to be marked. Hips that gently slope to full, beautiful thighs, a pussy with a matching silk thong I want to rip between my teeth. She has the smallest heart tattoo on her left hip, and her little toenails are painted red.

"You're beautiful," I say truthfully. Before she can respond, I cross the room to her, weave my hands through that mane of chestnut, tug her head back, and take her mouth in mine. This is no gentle lover's kiss. Her lips are soft and taste sweet as honey. She wraps her arms around my shoulders and neck, and I pull her torso flush against my body. I kiss like this is the last night we have. Like it's the first kiss she's ever gotten and I want it to be memorable. Like tomorrow might not come. My dick's hard against her belly. I cup her ass and she moans. With effort, I pull away.

"I've been thinking about that spanking all day, daddy," she breathes. "I need more."

"Bed," I rasp out. "Get on your knees for daddy."

She obeys, scrambling to her knees. I slap her ass and gently push her belly down. "That's a girl," I say, when her back arches. She puts her hands directly out in front of her and the curve of her ass begs for another swift spank. "Very good girl. Not so good she didn't earn herself an ass whipping," I say, chiding her. I reach for the clasp of my belt and unfasten it. With a whir and tug, I pull it through the loops.

She whips her head around and looks to the side at me, her eyes wide and curious, but she doesn't lose her position. I double the belt in my hands, pull the end and *snap!* Her fingers tighten on the bedspread as I rear it back, then swing the leather against her naked skin, the thong doing nothing to protect her from the strap. A red mark blooms on her gorgeous skin and she yelps a little, then falls right back into position and arches her back.

She wants more. Harder.

I whip her again with the belt, stripe after stripe

landing in criss-crossed red marks across her ass. "You gonna be a good girl for daddy?" I ask her, before I deliver half a dozen more vicious swipes of the best.

"Yes, daddy," she moans.

"If I touched your sweet pussy right now, would I find you wet for daddy?"

She groans and whimpers, rocking her hips a little. "Soaked."

She's so damn unencumbered. God, I need to fuck this woman and make my claim. I give her three more hard licks with the belt, each swish and *thwack* making me harder. I let it fall to the floor and take a condom out of my wallet.

"You need daddy's cock in that pussy," I grit out. She looks over her shoulder at me and nods with vehemence.

"Please," she begs.

I unfasten my jeans and take out my swollen cock, slide the condom on, then come up behind her. I take her hair and let it tumble over her shoulders, bring my mouth to her ear and whisper. "I fuck hard, princess. It's how I like it. But I know you can take it."

She grins and says the one thing that'll make me even harder. "Yes, daddy."

I position behind her and line my cock up at her entrance. I moan at the feel of her hot pussy on my cock head. I tease the very edge of her pussy, draw myself across her clit, slide up and down her channel, teasing her. She moans and wriggles her hips, but I slap her ass. My handprint blossoms on her skin. I anchor myself on her hips and plunge into her to the hilt. Fuck, she's tight and hot and wet. My vision blurs, and I groan.

"Jesus," I curse. "Fucking *Christ.*"

She pushes back against me and I spank her again. "Chest down," I bark out, keeping her in place by fisting my fingers in her hair and tugging at the scalp, muttering filthy oaths, and my words are lost as I plunge into her again and again. She's arching her back, ready to climax, her fingers gripping the bedsheets.

"Come," I order her. "Let yourself go."

A slow moan builds to a bigger crescendo. She's whimpering and shifting and panting. I slam into her again and again, until I'm ready to blow. Her orgasm tears through her and she screams. Her head's thrown back, her forehead dotted with perspiration. The sound of her coming pushes me right over the edge and I chase my own ecstasy with her name on my lips. I come hard and fast, groaning into her ear.

We slump to the bed exhausted and sated. I bend down and brush a kiss against her temple. Her eyes are closed and she's smiling.

"Seriously amazing," she whispers. "I've never experienced anything like that before in my life."

I run my fingers through her hair. "Never? Are you fucking kidding me?"

She smiles. "Not everyone fucks like that, Levi. Seriously. This comes as a surprise to you?" She's giggling. I reach down and tickle her side which makes her laugh out loud.

"And not everyone fucks like *you*." I tell her. So goddamned receptive to my belt. My deepest fantasies involve whipping off my belt and striping an ass like hers, then fucking her from behind with her heated, spanked ass pressed up against me. She opens one eyes and looks up to me.

"Legit?"

That makes me laugh out loud. "Legit."

"Well," she says thoughtfully. "We'll have to do that again sometime."

I bend down and kiss her temple again. "We do."

I pull out of her, noting that she whimpers a little. The princess likes my cock in her pussy. Jesus, she's perfection. I clean her up then sling my jeans on and pad into her kitchen bare-chested.

She comes into the kitchen wearing my t-shirt, and it's all I can do not to push her up against this counter and fuck her again. We'll get there.

"You hungry?" I ask her.

"Starving. Like not even kidding you. I've had nothing but M&M's and coffee today."

I turn and raise an eyebrow at her. "What the hell?"

She shakes her head. "For real. You like Indian?"

I shrug. "I like food. Don't much care what it is."

"Perfect." She grabs a stack of menus she's got attached to her fridge with a magnetic clip. "Let's get Indian. It's fast and delish."

We hang in her kitchen and chat. She's still standing there with mussy, just-fucked hair and her nipples poking straight through my t-shirt and I'm leaned up against her counter, barefoot with nothing but jeans on. It's weirdly comfortable and doesn't feel like the one-night stand it's meant to be.

Thirty minutes later, we've got several white boxes and a few wax paper bags with flat bread things.

"What the fuck's that?"

"Naan," she says with a grin. "Try it."

I actually like it even though I've never had it before. She chows down on chicken with a spicy yellowish-orange sauce and little triangle-shaped things stuffed with veggies, and I eat everything she serves me. We talk comfortably. I guess there's something about bandaging up a girl's wound, having her call me daddy, spanking her ass and fucking her soundly that'll bring a couple closer together or some such shit.

Doesn't matter. Fuck one night stands. We'll make this a two-week stand and then go our separate ways.

Whatever it is, I like it.

We clear the table and she puts the leftovers away. I rinse her dishes and put them in her dishwasher in amicable silence.

"Are you…hanging around for a while?" she asks.

"Well, I'm a little worried about that cut on your hand," I say to her, running a hand through my hair. Her hand's fine and we both know it. I give her a wink. She bites her lip. And the next thing you know, she's up in my arms with her legs wrapped around my waist. I'm holding her by the ass and backpedaling her to her bedroom, my dick straining for release against my jeans, her full ass pressed up against me.

I drop her on the bed. She bounces and looks up at me, her eyes bright. I kneel down, one leg on either side of her, capture her wrists, and pin them above her head, then lower my mouth to hers and kiss her long, slow, and deep, a silent conversation that needs no more words than this. I've had one night stands and I've fucked women whose names I didn't even know, but this? This is different. She's holding nothing back for me, and I can tell just by the way she is now that this is new territory for her. I love that. She's never been taken like this. Loves being dominated. And fuck if I don't want to give her exactly what she needs.

When I pull my mouth off hers, she whispers, "you're my boss, though. There's something a little taboo about this."

"In two weeks, I'm firing you," I tell her.

She grins. "I don't have much incentive to behave myself, then, if I'm already getting fired."

"You forget those spankings? Maybe you need another reminder."

"Fuck," she groans. Then her hands are scrambling at the shirt and my hands are fumbling at my jeans and we're ready for round two. This time I hold her wrists above her when I slide into her sweet, soft folds. This time she closes her eyes when she arches her back, her ecstasy matching mine when we both chase our release. I tumble beside her sweaty and sated and panting when my phone buzzes.

"Son of a bitch," I mumble at the same time she says, "my car!"

And sure as fuck, when I answer the phone, it's Grease.

"Where is she?" he asks. For a second I wonder why the fuck he wants to know where she is, when I realize he's asking because he needs to know her address to drop her car off. Jesus, I have to get my shit together.

Do I want to keep us together a secret?

"Just a minute." I hit mute just to be safe and look over at her.

She whispers her address, I give it to him, then I shut the phone off and lay down beside her. With a sigh, she hitches a leg up on my mine and lies her head on my chest, like it's the normal, natural thing to do. Snuggling. I don't snuggle with girls but with Tanya, I'll give it a go.

"Could complicate things," I tell her.

"Yeah," she says, her eyes closed already. "I mean there's the whole *friends with benefits* thing. A boss with benefits though?"

We'll just have to play it carefully. I'm not worried about my employees. I've got nothing to hide. Her father, though. That's another story.

"If your father catches wind I'm working on his car, there'll be hell to pay," I remind her. "If he finds out I'm fucking his *daughter*."

She opens her eyes. "Ok so the last thing I want to talk about right now, when I'm lying next to you, and I just screamed your name when I came, is my *father.*" She grins and tugs at the hair on my chest, flashing me a coy grin. "I'd rather just talk to my *daddy.*"

I chuckle and give her hair a little tug. "I like that."

She sobers and places her hand flat on my chest. "I'm glad…daddy." Her cheeks are flushed, but I'm not sure if it's a post-sex glow or she's embarrassed.

"You're a good girl," I say. "Gotta to make sure your car's okay."

I get dressed to head downstairs so it doesn't look too suspicious when Grease shows up with the car. Before I leave, I disable the thumbprint recognition on the door so I can come back in and not disturb her. She's tired. Probably the first day the girl's worked like this, and she's wiped. Plus I like the idea of coming back to her still in bed.

For a little while, when I was tucked up in all things Tanya, I forgot that she's in a fucking penthouse. That the elevator doors gleam with their mirrored interiors, and a goddamn chandelier hangs in the foyer. When I step off into the main area, a couple stops and stares. The man's wearing a black three-piece suit. He's clean-shaven and balding, with gray hair at his temples and a receding hairline. The woman wears a black evening gown, with silver sequins around her neck, and her jewelry is so heavily laden with diamonds she's practically blinding me. She scowls at me as I step off the elevator, and her husband peers down his nose at me in my work clothes and tats.

I never really care what people think, but it's a reminder to me that this is Tanya's crowd. Her father is one of them. They scorn blue collar laborers like me. I scowl right back at the bitch in a gown and tip an imaginary hat to her. Jesus. Like money makes you better than anyone else. I own the most well-established fucking classic car shop in America for Christ's sake, and I know the value of my assets and inventory. I earned every fucking penny myself, unlike half of these idiots who had it handed to them. I just don't go around flaunting money like a goddamned sheik.

The woman in the gown huffs out indignantly and mutters something to her husband about "better security" and "lapses in judgment." I ignore her and keep walking. I do turn heads with these damn tats in a place like this, which is maybe a strategical error. Fuck that.

And as I go into the street and flag Grease down, I show him where to park her car in the lot, and I wonder to myself. Will there be a next time? Or is this a one-off?

When I get back to the apartment, I let myself in the apartment. I toss her keys on the counter, kick my shoes off, and let myself really look at her place.

Her living room is decorated in shades of blue and white, like a beach-themed retreat. It's pleasing to the eye and comfortable looking, not severely modern or desperately country and homespun, but something in between. It's clean but not impeccable. She's got a stack of magazines on the coffee table, a laundry basket with folded yoga pants and tops, and a shitload of plants on a window with some leaves strewn around the bases. A pile of blankets sits on one sofa, and her desk has a stack of papers on it. I walk to the desk, eyeing the framed prints curiously. Is it her family? Siblings? From where I stand I can't see them.

I walk closer and feel my eyes go wide. Wow. They're all...her. But they're not candid shots taken at family vacations, but professionally done. She's wearing a bikini in one on the beach, and in another she's holding a man's hand. I frown. Who the fuck is that? He's got a polo shirt on and cargo shorts, and the two of them are standing at the beach like they're models for a surf club.

Models? I frown, turn back and go to her room. Is she a model?

Is she…single?

Maybe something I should've found out before I fucked her senseless.

I stand in the doorway and look in. She's dead asleep, her arm strewn over her head like a carefree child. She's beautiful and sweet like this. I'll find out what I need to tomorrow. I tuck the blanket in around her.

"Get some sleep, princess," I whisper. "You've got work early tomorrow, and your boss doesn't like latecomers."

I scrawl a note on her desk, and head home.

Chapter Seven

Tanya

I wake sometime in the middle of the night and realize he's gone. I should have expected it, but I still don't like it. It makes me feel sort of cheap that he just fucked me and left me like that, but I guess it's probably best this way. I mean, I'm me and he's…him, and there's no way anything between us could ever be more than a quick fuck. It saddens me but I'm so tired I roll over and fall right back asleep until my alarm rings the next morning.

I glance at my phone, but there's no message. Does Levi use a cell phone? I realize I've never seen one in his hands.

My ass aches from the spanking—no, *spankings*—he gave me, and I'm sore from being fucked by him. I should be maybe embarrassed to see him today. Like a normal girl would be ashamed. I called him daddy, bent over his desk for a spanking, and fucked him in my own bed. I'm not, though. I don't regret a damn thing. I haven't had sex like that in…well, ever.

I shudder when I remember sex with Leon. He talked

incessantly, and it wasn't the pleasant kinda filthy talk I want to hear but sorta creepy. I really don't need a play by play about every single move a guy's gonna make in bed, how hard he is, and exactly when he's planning on coming. He was in good shape and was decent enough, but sex was…lackluster. And weird.

Last night, though. Last night was a night to remember.

Today I pick a somewhat more sensible outfit that I can work in that still looks good. A designer dark-washed denim skirt with a fitted, olive-colored top with a delicate picot edge and sturdy but still cute ballet-flats. Casual but nice. I twist my hair into a long, long braid and let it hang over my shoulder, then grab a pair of gold hoops. It's a lot simpler than my usual clothes, but I've got work to do. It isn't until I'm making my bed that a note flutters to the floor I hadn't seen before. I pick it up and smile to myself.

Good morning, princess. Get yourself some breakfast and meet me at the shop early. I'd like to give you a good morning kiss, and your boss might not be happy if you're late. Your car's in your assigned spot, keys on the counter. xx Levi

My heart flutters in my chest and I smile. Well that was cute. Funny, when I first met him the word *cute* didn't seem to go with his growly nature at all, but now… I shake my head. Nothing can happen between us, so it won't be smart for me to start getting all heartsick and shit over this. I have two weeks with him and hell, I'm going to make the most of it. Nothing real will ever happen between us. It can't. But who says we can't enjoy two weeks together?

It's sorta sweet he told me to make sure I get some breakfast. I like that. It's like he's watching out for me or something.

I don't have much in the way of breakfast foods here, so I hit the coffee shop before work and grab myself a bagel with a veggie cream cheese shmear, and a box of muffins for the guys. I park my car and head in, and it isn't until I'm standing in front of the door with a box of muffins

in one hand, my paper bag holding my bagel dangling precariously on top, and a steaming hot cup of coffee in the other, when I realize I still don't actually have a key to let myself in.

"Son of a bitch," I mutter, attempting to push the door open with my hip, which proves impossible since it's locked. Coffee sloshes onto my hand in the process. I curse and step back, raising my eyes heavenward. I'm starting to mutter something about how Levi could maybe think to get me a key, when the familiar gritty voice makes me jump and slosh coffee all over my hand again.

"Morning."

"*Jesus*, you scared the hell out of me," I tell Levi, leveling an angry look at him.

He raises a dark brow and frowns. "Good morning to you, too." And just like that, my body knows how to respond. This man pushed me over his desk and spanked me yesterday, then took his leather belt to my ass before he fucked me so hard and thoroughly I slept in a sex-induced coma. And my body knows this. So at the sound of the stern tone and raised brow, at the first sign of his familiar dominance, my body starts to react. I push my thighs together at the thrum of arousal, and swallow hard, trying to maintain my composure.

He circles me, which makes me feel decidedly helpless while I'm holding the box of muffins and bagel with the screaming hot cup of coffee. Eyeing the white box, he mutters, "Lake's Coffee Shop."

"Mmhmm. Now, sir," I say with a tight voice mimicking patience I'm sure as hell not feeling at the moment, "will you please open the door for me?"

He shrugs lazily. "I'm not sure yet."

My mouth hangs open, agape. "What?"

Stroking his chin methodically, he nods. "Yeah. I think I'd be a dumbass not to take advantage of this situation."

"Levi! Leave me alone now. Just open the door and I won't bother you. But for God's sake, have some mercy." I chatter on, trying to convince him, but he just continues his pacing unhindered.

He circles around me again, but this time I gasp when I feel his hand on my ass. "Still hot from last night," he approves. "Perfect."

"Someone will hear you," I hiss.

"You're the one doing all the talking," he counters. His hand snakes under my skirt and rakes his hand up my thigh. My legs quiver, my pussy throbs. Flicking his thumb over the teeny strip of fabric between my legs, he brings his mouth to me ear. "Do not," he says, punctuating his words with firm but gentle pressure of his thumb, "wear panties to this office again. If you do, and I find them, I'll punish that sweet pussy of yours before I punish your ass. Understood?"

Jesus Christ, he's filthy.

I love it.

He gives my inner thigh an almost affectionate pinch.

"Ow!" I protest, splashing coffee on my hand again. "You made me spill my coffee."

Taking my coffee-burned hand in his, he brings it to his lips, kissing the reddened part. "Sorry about that, Tanya," he says. "Let daddy kiss it better." And just like that, I melt into a puddle of Tanya goo, right there on the front step.

"Thank you, daddy," I whisper, instantly forgiving him for whatever was irritating me before. I don't care if anyone hears us. I don't care if anyone sees us. I want him to touch me more, to bring me into that shop and kiss me more. To let me call him *daddy* again.

Letting my hand go, he takes his key from the loop on his belt and opens the door, then turns and plucks the box of muffins and coffee from my hands. "In you go," he says, holding the door open for me. I incline my head to thank him, step over the threshold, then squeal when he gives my ass a little swat.

Is it still only seven in the morning? I'm ready to bed this guy already. God, I'm a slut.

The door shuts behind us and he leads me to the desk. He puts the muffins down and places my coffee on the desk. I'm wondering why he just divested me of my coffee when he reaches for me around the waist and pulls me between his legs. Strong, powerful fingers dig through my hair, rough and unrepentant, and my braid begins to come undone. Tugging my head back, he brings his mouth to mine and kisses me so that my knees buckle. He holds me up and kisses me harder, deeper, his tongue gently probing mine, but the fist in my hair only tightens every time our tongues meet. I moan into his mouth. His cock presses hard against my belly. I don't care if anyone sees us. I can't stop this if I tried. He was meant to kiss me like this, right here and right now, and I'm letting myself be swept away in this moment. Too soon, he pulls away. I blink at him with hazy eyes, my lips swollen and tingling.

If I had even an inkling of doubt he's interested in me, they just vanished.

"What was that?" I whisper.

"It was a good morning, princess," he grates.

I finger his swollen cock through his jeans. "And that?"

He grins, white teeth flashing behind dark, thick whiskers. "Think that's saying the same thing."

I bite my lip and he groans. Running my thumb up and down his shaft, I lean in and whisper in his ear, "I had fun last night, daddy. I was sad to see you gone this morning."

Running his thumb along my cheek, he cups my jaw and whispers back, "Maybe tonight I don't have to leave. But Tanya," he says, his voice deepening in warning. "Stop teasing me. If I have to work today with blue balls hanging between my legs because of you, I'll have to punish you later."

I moan. "You'll have to find another way to get me to behave. That's only turning me on." I lean in and lick his collar bone. "I wanted to make myself come this morning imagining you bending me over the hood of one of those cars and fucking me soundly."

"*Christ*," he curses, with a groan.

We pull away at the sound of footsteps approaching, and by the time Spade comes into the office, I'm dutifully sipping my coffee and eating my bagel, and Levi's leaned up against the counter spilling blueberry muffin crumbs all over the place.

"Morning, boss," Spade says. The acrid scent of cigar smoke hits me, and my bagel churns in my stomach. I can't stand this guy. He jerks his chin to me. "Morning…Anya?" His lewd gaze sweeps down my front, undressing me with his eyes.

"Tanya," I say through gritted teeth. "Would you like a muffin?"

Without so much as a thank you, he reaches in and grabs two chocolate chip muffins. He heads to the shop, spraying crumbs as he goes.

"Screw muffins," I mutter, scowling at the flurry of crumbs everywhere. "Next time, I bring a fruit tray."

Levi nods and shoots me a wink that goes right to my nipples.

Jacked Up

Fuck, I'm toast.

I need to busy myself before I start undressing myself right here in front of him, so I find the utility closet and a broom, because I just remembered there's broken glass on the floor from the night before.

"Hey," I say, when I come to the desk and see no broken glass. "What happened to the mess that was here last night?"

He shrugs. "I came and cleaned it up before I went home. I didn't like the idea of you coming in this morning to it."

I smile. "How very...*daddy* of you."

Leaning in, he gives me a parting kiss, then whispers into my ear before he goes, "Some time today, before we close shop for the night, those panties are mine. Bring them to me. If I close shop and you're still wearing them, I'll redden that ass when we're through here."

And with that, he's gone. I'm chewing my bagel without conscious thought, trying to keep my shit together before anyone comes in, but all I can do is imagine myself lying over his lap or sprawled on the bed waiting for him as he gets ready to take me from behind. Ha. So this is part of his plan? Forget sexting. I've got a boss with a filthy mind who apparently likes to keep me on my toes while I'm working.

Well, two can play at that game.

I finish my bagel and wad up the wrapper, toss it into the wastebasket by the desk, and make myself a small agenda for today.

Answer phones.
Check supplies in bathrooms.
Respond cheerfully to customers.
Annoy the hell out of boss.

The phone rings and I answer it promptly in my best

Eastern European accent in case my father decides to shave years off my life again. "Jacked Up Classic Auto Repair, how may I be of assistance?"

"Well, what a pretty voice you have," says a warbly, somewhat reedy voice on the other end. "Has Levi finally climbed off his pile of gold and broken down and hired help?"

Pile of gold? The tone is friendly, though, and the man sounds like he's about a hundred years old.

"Why, yes, sir," I respond, in the same accent. "I believe he has. May I tell him who's calling before he climbs back up his pile?"

The man cackles out loud, "I like you. You're feisty, like your boss. From what country do you hail from, young lady?"

Shit. I hadn't thought that through.

"Czechoslovakia," I blurt out. My cheeks flame. I'm going to have to come up with some sort of back story, or someone will figure me out. Damn it.

He clears his throat, "You mean The Czech Republic, or Slovakia? I believe we stopped calling it Czechoslovakia about twenty years ago." His reedy, thin voice sounds amused.

"Oh, right. Vell…old habits," I mutter.

I can practically hear him smiling.

"So vhat can I do for you?" I ask, fighting to keep the accent by adding a few rolled "r's" in for good measure.

He leaves a message for Levi, and when I hang up the call, four more calls come in, one after the other. I file the messages, organizing the desktop on his computer, sync all files with the cloud drive, and dust the display case before I realize it's nearly lunchtime. Levi hasn't come back in the office, and I'm doing a shit job keeping those blue balls primed. I bite my lip and grin to myself when I get an idea.

A few minutes later, I've got a slew of cleavage shots on my phone ready to go. As a professional model, I know how to do this.

Problem is, I don't have his cell phone number. I eye the door to the shop. I remember that threat of a bare ass spanking. I bite my lip. Yeah, that sounds hot as fuck, but do I really want to play it from that angle? And is it really hot if he's *really* mad?

I peer through the glass door into the shop and notice the men are all leaving for lunch. I hit the button on the phone that sends all calls to voicemail. Turning to face the door, I take a deep breath and square my shoulders. I haven't seen Levi since early this morning. Is he still here? Would he leave without telling me?

I frown to myself, but I guess it's fine if he did. I mean, I don't mean much to him.

I open the door, stand on the threshold, but move my feet to the side so I'm still in the office and can make a good argument for not breaking the rule. "Levi?" I yell out. At first I don't hear anything and I wonder if he's gone to lunch alone. Would he do that? Just leave for lunch and not even say anything to me? I frown. I thought I deserved at least a little recognition. I try again. "Levi?"

"Yeah?" he calls out, his voice muffled.

"There's a customer that needs to talk to you. Do you have a cell phone number I can have?"

He rattles off a number. With a little smile, I run back into the shop, pick up my phone, and send him the pictures. I grin to myself. That'll get him back for getting handsy outside the damn shop.

I go back to the doorway and step right on the edge again like before.

I hear a rustling sound and look into the shop. I tumble inside, then quickly right myself and leap back so my feet are back in the office. I'm off balance, though, so I'm swaying like a hula-hoop dancer when Levi pushes himself out from under a car about ten feet away to the far right. It's a beautiful, pale blue car with a long, flat hood. Silver chrome trim, like ribbon on a present, decorates the outside. I can kinda see the appeal of working with cars like this.

Levi sits up. In his right hand he's got some kind of a drill. He pushes safety goggles up on top of his head and frowns at me.

"What'd I tell you about coming into this shop?" he asks in a stern half-growl that makes my nipples furl.

I give him my most winsome grin. "I'll have you know I'm not in the shop. If you'd look more closely, you'll see the very bottom of my flats are *still* on the threshold of the door," I say with triumph.

Still scowling, he pushes himself to standing, and that's when I notice he's stripped to his white t-shirt rolled up to his shoulders, the stark brightness in contrast to his tanned, tattooed arms. Placing the drill on a table beside him, he now has two free hands which he plants on his hips to further the impact of his frown.

"Safety regulations per order of the insurance company state no one inside the doorframe of that door are allowed in here unless they work in this shop," he barks out. "And *daddy's* rules are even stricter."

Shit.

"I work—" I gesture wildly behind me. "...in the shop." I set myself off balance and topple straight into the shop, but quickly scurry back.

"Get back into that office," he rumbles, advancing on me now.

Jacked Up

Uh oh. I maybe pushed this a little too far. I run over to the desk but he's here now. Damn it. I didn't even get to really provoke him and he's coming at me like he's a dog whose dinner I just stole. There's literally nowhere for me to go, so I sorta sidestep and bolt for the door, but he catches me around the waist.

"Wait!" I yell, trying to wriggle, but he's really crazy strong. He's pushing me up against the wall. His whole body is still sweat-slicked so the white t-shirt clings to him like a second skin. He shoves me up against the wall so the cool, flat surface presses up against my spine. With one knee he pins me against the wall. He has both of my hands in one of his huge ones, pinned above my head, and the other one comes to my jaw.

"I don't think you got my point, princess," he says. His breath brushes my cheeks, minty and cool, and I shiver. I remember what this man did to me last night. My body does, too. My ass tingles and belly contracts at the memory.

"I got your point," I tell him, and flash him a smile. "Daddy."

Still frowning, he raises a stern brow at me. "Did you just talk back?"

"Of course not. I wouldn't do that."

If he's amused, he's not letting on. "Tanya," he warns.

I bite my lip and swallow. He lets my wrists go, takes a step back, and stands with his arms folded on his chest. "Go shut and lock the door," he says ominously. Oh, boy. So he's going to stand there and watch me do it? I make sure my ass sways a little as I walk on these freaking amazing flats to the door, swing it shut, and flip the bolt.

"Have you checked your phone lately, daddy?" I ask him with a low, seductive purr.

His brows draw together. "My phone?"

"Mmhmm." I keep my hands tucked behind my back so I look like a good girl. "Your phone." I should maybe be a little self-conscious about the fact that I texted him boob shots, but seriously, the guy had his hands everywhere in broad daylight, so I have no regrets.

He's eyeing me curiously, though. "I don't have a phone," he says. "There's just a shop one we all use with the shop number on it."

I freeze. Someone's just dumped ice down my back.

"Holy shit," I say in a horrible, choked whisper, "tell me you know where that phone is."

Realization dawns on him at the tone of my voice and his eyes go to little, dangerous slits. "What the fuck did you do, Tanya?"

"Where's the phone?" I croak.

He growls. "Spade has it. Went out to get tires on his lunch break at a dealer we know. Took the phone in case another call comes in we're waiting on." He bends a finger at me. "What did you do?"

"Find him," I whisper with a groan. I slap my forehead. "Do you have something that can drive *fast* and not these old granny cars or that lumpy truck of yours? Oh! My car! I'll drive. Just tell me where to go."

I already have my keys out and I'm at the door.

"*Wait.*"

"I can't wait! Are you crazy? I need to get that damn phone before someone else does! Oh, God, I'm such an *idiot.*" I look over my shoulder at him and wag a finger in his direction. "In fact, you should probably spank me for this."

He huffs out a totally mirthless laugh. "You still haven't told me what you sent, and believe me, princess, that's *already* a given." My heart thumps and my panties dampen but I can't really think about that because I'm trying not to freak out. *This isn't about sex*, I tell myself.

Ha. *Suuuure*.

I just texted my boobs to the *creepiest guy ever* who I'm going to work with for the next two weeks. I deserve whatever I've got coming to me.

"I know where Spade is," he says. "If I call him, and tell him why I'm calling, he'll open up that fucking phone."

"Yes he will," I say through gritted teeth. "Ow!"

I yelp when his palm connects with my ass. "I cannot believe you fucking did that," he says, real anger in his look now that what I did really dawns on him. "You so need your ass paddled for that."

"I know," I groan. "I'm an idiot."

His hand comes to my neck and lightly tightens, just enough of a squeeze. "You don't go there, Tanya."

"Where?"

"No idiot comments. You did something stupid I'm gonna spank your ass for later, but for now, keep your head on straight and we'll find that damn phone. Got it?"

I sigh, a lump rising in my throat that surprises me. "Yeah," I whisper. He releases me, and I head to the driver's side. He blocks me and takes my keys.

"Funny, baby," he says, without any actual indication that he's amused. "So cute you think I'll let you drive when you're all worked up like this."

It comes as no surprise he won't let me drive right now. Honestly, I wouldn't be surprised if he *never* lets me drive, he's just that bossy. I hand him my keys with trembling hands, go to my side, buckle in, and we're off.

"How far is it?" I ask, wringing my hands.

"Not far," he says. He's still angry. I can feel it emanating off him like embers burning in a fire, slow and steady but blisteringly hot. "And by the way, after we get this phone, you have the rest of the day off."

My heart sinks. Ugh. It's like he's temporarily firing me.

"Are you letting me go because I acted unprofessionally?" I ask, feeling little and small.

He turns to look at me and shakes his head, then looks back at the road. "No, babe," he grits out. "But I need to take a look at what you sent. Then, I'm gonna wipe the phone. If he *did* see what you sent, I wanna make sure none of them lay eyes on you. If they didn't, we have some business to deal with before you step foot back in that office."

I cross my arms on my chest and pout a little.

"Are you pouting?"

"Hmmph," I say in return.

He reaches over and squeezes my knee. "You're pouting."

"I'm not pouting," I lie, trying to move away from him but unlike his truck that's big enough I could lay out on the bench and sunbathe, there's no room in this little cab for me to move away from him.

"Tell daddy if you're pouting," he says, his gravelly voice just a tad bit sweeter when he adds the *daddy*.

Mmm.

"Maybe a little," I say. "I just. This is awful. Let's just get this over with."

"We will," he says. "Promise."

He pulls up to a place with a large sign out front, silver awning with glass windows housing all sorts of car repair things.

"You stay here," he says, which I'm grateful for. When he goes in, I'll maybe find a rock to crawl under. I close my eyes and lay my head back on the seat, just waiting for him to finish. A few minutes later, he's back, and he's holding a cell phone triumphantly in his hand, but he still looks grim.

"You got it?" I ask when he opens the door.

"I did," is all he says. He shuts the door and starts the car.

"Oh, God. Did he look at the picture?" I ask.

"Says he didn't, and I think he's telling the truth because he's a really shit liar," he says. "Plus the phone was still on the console in the car."

"Then why do you look so...like, stern or something?" I ask.

With a low rumbling growl, he pulls into the intersection and starts heading to the street.

"Where are we going? Levi?" This isn't the way to my place.

He growls again.

"Um, daddy?"

"Because *I* fucking looked at the picture," he says in a choked, tight voice. "And the idea of *anyone else* looking at that makes me want to..." his voice trails off and he clenches his jaw. "Jesus Christ," he finally mutters.

Oh boy. This is not good.

"We've only known each other like a day," I say, totally unhelpfully because that only earns me a silent glare.

Lovely.

He's driving out of the city now, but not far. I've never been out this way.

"We're not going back to the shop," I say with wonder.

He shakes his head. "You think I want to take the chance of one of them seeing you when I bare your ass?"

I make a sort of strangled noise, which just earns me another raspy grunt.

The streetlights are further apart and the houses are nice, but separated from each other by large distances. We pull in front of a large, rambling house, with a front porch and a massive golden dog curled up on the porch.

"Welcome to my place," Levi says, still stern and growly but now a little proud.

So he's brought me to his place. This feels special somehow, like he doesn't do something like this often. Then I remember he's mad at me, and I try to keep the excitement down. Is he mad?

There's a garage to the side but the doors are shut, and I wonder what's inside. I suspect I have a good idea, though, and maybe he'll tell me. When we get up on the porch two more dogs come around the corner and they all greet Levi with excited wags of their tails. Something flutters in my heart, and I smile to myself. His place is more welcoming than mine, the smell of fresh pine and basil from a plant on the front stoop filling my senses.

Levi opens the front door and lets me in, holding it for me. I step into his house, and my eyes open in wonder. It's nothing at all like I'd expect from a guy like him. It's a large, spacious farmhouse, with worn, comfortable furniture, bookshelves upon bookshelves housing books of every shape and color, handspun carpets on the floors and multicolored blankets piled in on a rocking chair in front of a large fireplace.

This is Levi's home?

"This," I say with wonder, looking all around me. "Is *not* the type of place I'd expect a guy like you to live in."

"No?" He crosses his arms and leans against a gleaming chestnut-colored mantle. "What would you expect from a guy like me?"

I wrinkle up my brow and think. "Well, honestly, I have no idea," I have to admit. "Legit none. But I sort of imagined like an abandoned warehouse or something, I guess. Metal walls. Concrete floors."

Jacked Up

"Sounds comfy," he says with a laugh. Then he pushes off the wall and stalks over to me. I stand there like an idiot, because what else am I going to do?

He's either going to spank me or fuck me and I'm not sure which one I want him to do. Preferably both.

When he reaches me, he takes me by the upper arm and holds tight. There's a large blue sofa that looks big enough for the two of us to sleep in if we wanted to. He folds his large frame into one corner, and drags me over. He plunks me onto his lap, wraps one large hand around the back of my neck and tips my head back so he can kiss me. It's a quick, rough kiss, his whiskers scraping my sensitive skin.

"God, you're beautiful," he says. "Those pictures made me hard as a fucking rock. Where were you when you took them?"

"Um. Bathroom at Jacked Up," I groan, because I know exactly what's going to happen next. He tips me to the side on his lap and slaps my ass, hard, with the flat of his hand.

"Told you I'd spank you bare," he rumbles. He bends me over his knee and hikes my skirt up. I'm dangling precariously over his knee and trembling because I know what's coming, and hell if I don't want it.

With a loud rending of fabric, he tears my panties right off me. "Time for those panties," he says. He folds them up and shoves them in his pocket. This is so damn wrong, but I'll die if he stops now.

"How many pictures did you send?" he asks.

"Six," I groan and brace for what I know's coming, and I'm not disappointed. He gives me six hard, searing smacks that take my breath away but light a fire in me. I squirm on his knee, so damn turned on I can't even think straight.

"Say, *I'm sorry, daddy,*" he instructs, hand perched precariously over my ass.

"I'm sorry, daddy," I say. My chest gets all tight when I call him daddy. I fucking *love* it.

Without a word he pushes his hand between my legs and starts touching, fondling, caressing me. I part my legs and pant over his lap.

"Good girl," he says, gently touching the edge of my channel. "Milk daddy's fingers like a good girl."

"Oh my God," I groan. I've never heard a guy talk dirty like this but I don't want him to stop. He impales me with his fingers. Shooting tremors of arousal shudder through me. I groan out loud, gyrating my pelvis on him.

"Good girl," he says. "Just like that, baby."

He's hard under my belly and I know he wants this badly, as badly as I want him.

"You're soaking daddy's fingers," he says. "Somebody likes getting her ass spanked."

"Daddy," I breathe, my need to come getting hotter, more intense. It's all I can think of.

"Come, babygirl," he orders, pumping into me harder and faster.

I let myself fly, chasing my ecstasy over his knee like he told me to. Something about the way he orders me to do this makes me want to laugh and cry and snuggle up on his chest all at once, like he's the one orchestrating my every emotion and need. I need this. *This.* I give myself over to the power of my climax coursing through me, and just when I'm coming down from the high, he positions me on the couch, my arms on the arm rest. I hear him unfasten his jeans and push them down. He's ripping open a condom and I'm so damn ready. He slams into me hard, yanks my head back, and the pain radiates on my scalp.

I gasp, hold onto the edge of the couch, and brace

myself as he thrusts into me harder, faster. He's got my whole braid wrapped around his fists and he pulls again. This braid was a good call, I think, in a delirium of pleasure and pain and ecstasy as I chase a second powerful orgasm that rips through me when he grunts his own release.

We're panting and sweating and somewhere in the distance a dog whines, probably wondering if he's half killing me.

"God, you make a slut out of me," I mutter, my eyes still closed. He slaps my ass affectionately.

"I might need to figure out a way to get you to work remotely," he grumbles. "I don't get a fucking thing done with you around."

We clean up and I pad out to the kitchen on bare feet. The kitchen's beautiful, with huge bay windows, a butcher block table, and stools covered with cushions in reds and blues. Copper pans hang from hooks on the wall, and open shelves house Mason jars of every shape and color. I love it.

I slide onto one of the stools as he goes to the fridge and takes out a pitcher of water. He pours me a glass and pushes it over to me. I take a sip, looking around his kitchen. He seems so out of place with his tats and black clothes, walking barefoot in a kitchen that looks like it could grace the centerfold in the Martha Stewart *Living* magazine. A large, thick red bowl with a fluted edge holds apples and oranges and lemons, beside a matching cutting board. He grabs a loaf of bread from somewhere, a bread knife, and cuts thick slices of crusty bread, which he piles on a large, sturdy plate. Everything about Levi is big and strong, so it fits that his home and the furnishings therein match that, I guess. Just like his truck.

He puts out a plate with wedges of white cheese, and

nudges over a bowl filled with dark purple grapes. My stomach growls.

"A post-sex feast," I mumble, taking a wedge of cheese with bread. The cheese is strong and creamy and my mouth waters. "Mmm."

"You like it?" he asks, turning back to the fridge and pouring himself a glass of water.

"Love it," I say, popping a few more grapes into my mouth.

A corner of his lips quirks up when one of the dogs pads into the kitchen. He bends down and scratches its ears.

"Didn't really peg you as a dog person," I say.

He looks up at me with a lopsided smile. "I think all your pegs for me were off the mark, princess. This is Murry."

I flush a little and nod. "Murry. I like that. And I think you're right…daddy."

It feels different calling him that now that we're sex-sated and eating an amiable lunch, but I wanted to test it out. His eyes warm appreciatively. He stands and leans against the counter. "You ever call a guy daddy?" he asks.

I shake my head. "No. I actually didn't even know it was a thing."

For some reason that makes him laugh. The deep rumble startles me, and I drop a grape that rolls onto the floor. Murry lunges for it but Levi snaps his fingers with a stern, "No."

The dog slinks back obediently and trots out the room.

"Wow. Even your dogs do what you say."

He looks at me curiously, like that's a weird thing to say. "Of course."

I smile. Naturally, it's a given for him.

"I dunno." I sigh, take another wedge of cheese, and

bring up what's bothering me. "So...you sure Slade didn't see that picture?"

The amusement on his face fades. He's scowling again. Great.

"I don't really want to talk about that again, Tanya," he says, but he shakes his head. "And no, he didn't. If I thought for a minute he did, I'd fire his ass."

I blink in surprise. "You'd fire an employee because he saw my boobs?"

His eyes darken. Walking over to me, he leans on the counter in such a way he's caging me in against it. I feel his heat again, and his voice has a visceral response on me when he starts talking. "I'd fire him a fucking minute if I thought he saw your tits," he says.

"But he works for you," I protest. "And you need him."

He shrugs a shoulder. "He's kind of a douchebag."

I smile. "Well, I'm glad he didn't see me. That was a really stupid thing I did. But you sort of provoked me."

Both of his brows shoot up in surprise. "Excuse me?"

"Well, you were the one with your hand up my skirt *in public* this morning," I mutter. I eat a whole fistful of grapes at once, so I don't have to speak for at least a few seconds. It's safer that way.

"So your response was to take a naked picture of yourself to get me back?"

Now that he says it that way, it sounds kinda stupid.

"Okay, so not my best strategic move."

He laughs. "Yeah. No."

We talk easily about anything and everything. Where he got the reclaimed wood on the floors of his kitchen, why he chose this house, how long he's been here and how many dogs he's adopted. My father and mother and the places I've traveled, what it's like being an only child and heir to my father's legacy.

"Have you all started on the car yet?" I ask.

He nods soberly. "Physically, not yet. The most important thing we do first is assess the damage and order parts that take a while to come. Once they're here, we begin work."

"Ah," I say. "Okay. And how long will this take?"

"Two weeks," he says. "More like twelve days now."

"So, just in time for me to get it back to my father before he's home."

"Yep," he says, clearly not amused, as his eyes are all narrowed again. "And just in time for me to get my shit done for the Fallside show."

I know that name. Why do I know that name?

"You alright, princess?" he asks.

"Yeah," I say. "I'm just trying to remember why I know that name."

He huffs out a breath. "Likely because your dad's ranked number one at that show for the past twelve years," he says.

Duh. I want to smack myself. *Of course* that's why.

How am I going to keep my cool at the show when I see Levi there? I have to go. I can't not go, now that I know he'll be there.

He tugs my braid and says, "I have to go back to work. You, however, are off for the rest of the day."

"Are you sure about that?" I ask him. "I was getting a lot done, you know."

"I'm sure about that," he says, fixing me with a serious look. "Better for me to focus on my work today, babe. And you're nothing but a distraction."

"Is that a compliment?" I ask. He just narrows his eyes. Alrighty then.

"How about I take you back," I say, "since your truck is at work. I get things done I need to, and then…" my voice trails off. I'm not sure if I'm much more than a fuck buddy to him. Does he want to see me tonight?

"Then I meet you at your place for dinner tonight," he says. "Okay?"

I smile to myself and nod. "Yes, daddy."

Chapter Eight

Levi

IT'S FUCKING hard to get my work done, even if she's *not* here. Part of me can't help but remember the way she felt when I buried myself in her. The feel of my palm marking her perfect, sweet ass. The taste of her mouth. And I sure as fuck wish I hadn't had to delete those pictures of her off my phone, because I'd do fucking anything to have those all to myself.

She hasn't come clean about the way she earns her money, but I'll ask her, and soon. I have my suspicions but don't want to assume.

Spade comes in and in typical asshole fashion, gives me shit about the phone.

"Something you don't want me to see on there, boss?" he asks with a chuckle.

"Yeah, dumbass," I tell him. "So mind your own fucking business."

I'm working through the voicemails that have come in

about the show in my absence and wondering why I did a stupid thing like give Tanya the day off. I even consider giving her a call and asking her to come back for an hour. I could use her help around here. Then I look at Spade's lewd grin and I know. Yeah, that's not happening.

I finish my work and call her on the office number. "I'll pick up dinner on the way, but I have a quick errand to run first, okay?"

"Sure," she says. "Do you want to eat at your place or mine?"

"Mine would be easier if you don't mind. I'll get a chance to walk the dogs instead of having to call my neighbor and ask her."

"Her?"

Is that jealousy?

What the hell are we playing at here? I've known her for such a short time, but in that time I've spanked her, kissed her, fucked her, and she's called me daddy. We're on the fast track to…something.

"Yeah. *Her*," I repeat. "The college student who's renting the house next door? She likes to pick up extra cash when she can."

"Hmph," she huffs out, clearly not impressed.

"Seven good?" I ask her.

"Perfect," she says.

We hang up, and for a minute I think to myself, this could be something more than it is. More than sex and fucking around with kink. God, she's so damn responsive. The way she moans, and the way she calls me daddy. Something tells me she'd be game for some of my kinkier persuasions.

But it's more than that. She's funny and sweet and witty. And the fucking nerve to text a picture like that. I shake my head. She's something else.

When I show up she's already there. Next to her in the car, I can't help but notice she's got a little duffle bag. It's pink and quilted with a golden handle, but it's not something that just sits in the car. She's packed a bag for the night.

She gets out with the bag in hand. I take the bag, lean in, and give her an affectionate kiss on the cheek.

"Been here long?" I ask her.

"Just got here. I was just admiring your view," she says, trotting to keep up with my long strides. I slow down for her, switch her bag and the one I'm carrying to my left hand, and take her by the right hand.

"I haven't even taken you to the back yet," I tell her.

"I was curious," she said. "Is that a barn?"

I nod. "Yep."

"Do you have, like…chickens or something?"

I tug her braid. "Or something. But first, dinner."

We make dinner like this is something that was meant to be. I slice tomatoes and mozzarella and she pulls fresh basil from the plant I have on the porch. We boil pasta and she tosses it with butter and sauce she finds in my cabinet. I never do normal shit like this with women, and I have to admit I like it.

"Missed you at the office," I tell her. "It was maybe rash of me to give you the rest of the day off. I really needed the extra help."

"Levi," she chides. "I'm going in early tomorrow, and I'll do what you need me to."

"You'll go in when I go in," I tell her. I don't like the idea of her there alone when it's dark.

She frowns. "Alright," she says, as if I've given her a choice.

I take her plate, lean down, and kiss her forehead. She's kicked off her shoes and came wearing jeans and a tank top. Damn if she doesn't look every bit as sexy in this outfit as she has in everything else I've seen her in.

"So what was your errand after work?" she asks. "And what's in the white paper bag?"

"Nosy little girl," I tell her, tugging her braid. "I'll show you."

I load the dishwasher and put the food away, then fetch the bag.

"After today, I realized I don't want to live in the dark ages anymore." I pull out the box with the brand new cell phone I picked up earlier today.

Her jaw drops. "You got a cell phone?"

I nod.

"Well, welcome to the twenty-first century," she says with a grin. "Can I play with it?"

"Play with it?"

"You know. Ringtones and wallpaper and stuff."

"No, I don't know," I tell her. "But yeah, I need you to help set it up. And then, when everything's done? I need you to text *me* those pictures."

She gives me a coy grin. "Only if you show me what's out back."

What she doesn't know is I was already planning that, so it's easy for me to pretend like I'm making a concession. "Alright," I tell her, adding some reluctance. "But be a good girl and only touch what I tell you to, okay?"

She tips her head to the side adorably. "Alien spaceship?" she guesses. When I shake my head, her voice drops. "Ohh. Is it where you show me your guns and knives and scary shit?"

I shake my head. "Nope."

"Horses? Big, beautiful stallions I can ride?"

"Nope," I tell her. "Now stop asking questions and lets go."

"Car things," she guesses, the closest guess yet. I smile and take her hand.

The sun is setting when we leave the house, wisps of pink and orange painting the horizon like someone drew a wide paintbrush across the sky. She pulls a little closer to me. I like this, having her so close, and for one minute I wonder what it would be like to have this be real. Not the temporary love affair that will vanish in days, but something lasting. I quickly push the thought away, though. I don't know her. Maybe she's on her best behavior now because I have something she needs, and she's got nothing else to do with her time.

But as we walk hand in hand toward the barn, in amicable silence, I let myself enjoy just being with her. I unfasten the series of padlocks one at a time. The door to the bar creaks open, and Tabby, the barn cat I keep that rids us of mice and critters, purrs and swoops between my legs. I give her an affectionate scratch behind the ears and she takes off.

Tanya lets go of my hand and lets loose a low, impressed whistle. Here in the barn, I keep my favorite possession, my pride and joy.

"She's beautiful," she breathes. "Levi…it's amazing. What kind of car is it?"

"It's a 1955 Jaguar D-type," I say. She slowly circles the car, letting her hand glide over the gleaming, deep blue sapphire finish. The sides slope downward to the windows. I've polished this until it glistens under the overhead lights. "It's a tail-finned racer, and one I've never taken to a show before."

"Wow."

"Fifty-four were made." I tell her. "It won Le Mans in 1956," I tell her. "Has a 285-horsepower inline six." I pat it affectionately. "It hit one hundred fifty-six miles an hour at

Jacked Up

peak. I don't race it anymore, though. Now, I baby her." I smile to myself. "No one else knows it yet, but I've got her registered at the next show."

"No way," Tanya says. "She's your prize?" She grins. "Oh my God, they're going to go nuts. But how did you *get* it? I mean, this thing's got to be worth…" her voice trails off. It's one of the most sought-after classic cars in the world. I've got her insured, but some would call me a fool keeping it in here like this.

"I inherited it from a friend of mine," I say. "Used to work with him. He was a neighbor growing up, and he taught me everything I know. Sal worked his whole life with cars, had no children, and decided when he was making out his will he wanted his cars to go to someone who'd appreciate them." I shrug. "It was the saddest day when Sal died. But that day changed my life." I inherited his business and this car, but I can't bring myself to show this one, not yet." I worked hard in my youth, earning Sal's trusts.

"Every penny I earned went toward my next car, and Sal was the one who gave me the space to store it. I bought this house when it went on the market. I couldn't imagine living anywhere else."

"Well that would explain why a tough guy like you lives in a place like this."

"Tough guy like me?" I ask with a chuckle.

She just shoots me a look that makes me smile. "Have you ever driven it?" she asks.

I grin. "Of course I have. What's the point if you don't get a chance to drive them every once in a while?"

She circles the car, nodding and admiring the details. It honestly gets me hard watching her take in my beauty. She appreciates my masterpiece. I love that she does.

"Ever kiss a girl in it?" she asks with a grin.

"I think that'd be uncomfortable," I tell her, eying the bucket seats that are meant for racing. But when she gets within arm's reach, I grab her about the waist and lift her onto the hood of the car. "But I can try the hood."

She grins, leans in, laces her hands around my neck, and I kiss her. She's soft and sweet and tastes delicious. My cock stirs to life when I take her mouth with mine and her body draws closer. I press my lengthened cock up against her, and her legs encircle me.

I pull my mouth off her.

"Baby," I whisper in her ear.

"Yes, daddy?"

Something in me draws even closer to her every time she calls me daddy. I fucking love that she does. Here, with my favorite possession I've shared with no one but Sal, holding her close and kissing her like this, I'm on top of the fucking world. We kiss until she moans into my mouth, her breasts pushed up against my chest. I pull my mouth off hers and whisper in her ear, "You want daddy to fuck that tight pussy, princess?"

She nods, her head bobbing up and down. "Daddy," she moans. "Please, daddy."

The car's just the right height. I unfasten my buckle, whip it off, and give the side of her thigh a quick smack with the leather before I toss it to the floor. She gasps and writhes, parting her legs. I hike her skirt up a little more and look at those beautiful legs spread wide on top of the bright blue hood of the car. Full, voluptuous thighs I want marked with my fingers under her skirt tomorrow. I hold her up, my thumbs pressed into her soft, sweet skin so hard I'm leaving red marks, but it only makes her moan harder.

"Fucking gorgeous," I groan, getting to my knees. "I want to taste that pussy. So every time I come in here and work on this car I think you. How you smell. How you feel. How you taste."

I part her knees. She gasps, panting now, when I kiss the inside of her thighs.

"Someone wants daddy to eat that pussy," I rasp out. Her skirt's up around her belly. She's naked from the waist down. I can smell her. My mouth waters. I breathe her scent in until I'm drunk with it, pull her pussy to my mouth, and work her hard and fast. She anchors herself on my hair, fingers wound tightly. Writhing against my mouth, she groans and comes so hard I have to hold her down while I milk her orgasm.

She's coming down in a haze, and I can't wait another minute.

"Tell me you've got protection," I growl.

She nods and mumbles about birth control, giving me the green light I want. I don't want to pause for a fucking condom. I need this girl ungloved. I hold her around the waist so hard she yelps, my fingers digging into her soft, sweet flesh.

"Daddy. God, yes, *daddy*," she moans. "Take me hard," she begs.

I thrust into her and she throws her head back, bracing herself on the hood of the car. A breeze rustles tendrils of hair on her forehead, her cheeks are dark pink and flushed. Her mouth parts while I take her, building a tempo of ecstasy.

"Fucking beautiful," I groan, slamming into her. Princess likes it hard, and today, I want to leave her bruised and soundly fucked. I groan into her, my orgasm tearing through me when she screams her ecstasy with me. "Good girl. That's it, baby." I push her damp hair off her forehead and kiss her flushed temple. She's panting on the car, boneless and replete. I hold her against me until her breathing slows, then I help her dress and we go to the house to clean up.

We walk hand in hand. She gets herself a glass of water and hands me a drink. I take the glass, take her fingers to my mouth, and kiss them. She smiles at me, her whole face lighting up. Beaming.

We say little after that, and I wonder if she's thinking what I am.

I'll never slake my need for her. Two fucking weeks isn't enough.

Chapter Nine

Tanya

EVERY DAY that ticks by on our two-week clock seems like the seconds of a time bomb. When my time here is up, there's nothing I can do to keep me a man like Levi. We're so wrong for each other and I know deep down inside it can't work out.

And what do we even have, anyway? Hot sex. Lots and *lots* of the hottest sex I've ever had in my life. What else do I have to offer him?

I haven't spent a night apart from him since that very first night. Some nights he stays at my place and some nights I stay at his. I have to admit, I prefer staying at his. Mine cost a mint and is decorated to perfection. I have my walk-in closet complete with designer labels and custom fitted clothing, enough shoes I could open a small boutique, and my bathroom filled with every possible beauty product I could hope for. Yet my place feels weirdly empty compared to his.

I put in a good day of work today, and Levi let me go early so I could prepare dinner while he finished a late job. He didn't know I was going to cook, though, just that I'd get something to eat. I have a small repertoire of food I make well,. I have a tray of baked, stuffed haddock browning in the oven, steamed green beans with slivered almonds warming in a pot on the stove, and I'm just fluffing the rice pilaf when he comes in the door.

"Smells like a goddamned restaurant in here," he says.

"Good," I say, welcoming him with a quick kiss over my shoulder, before I finish dinner. I squeal when he spins me around to look at him.

"Well ain't you pretty as a picture," he says in his deep rumble. My heart does a backflip when he weaves his hand around the hair I've got in a ponytail, gently tugs my head back, and makes my "welcome home" kiss look like a little girl dressed up in her mommy's nightie. His kiss is the whole enchilada, sending a shiver coursing right through me.

"Needed to kiss you properly," he says. "Come in my kitchen with you all dolled up in a frilly apron, you're lucky I don't fuck you right up against this fridge."

"The fish will be ruined," I breathe, sorta not caring if it is.

He chuckles, spins me around, and gives me an affectionate ass slap. "No ruining dinner, woman," he says. He's a freaking dinosaur but I love it.

I serve him his dinner which he inhales like he hasn't eaten since Christmas, takes my empty plate with a kiss to my forehead, then loads the dishwasher and tells me to take a break.

God, I could get used to this. A pang hits me in the chest. I've never had anything like this. I've spent my life bathed in luxury, but none of it matters. None of it at all.

Jacked Up

Here, Levi is exactly who he says he is. He's a man of his word, brutal and raw in his honesty. Hardworking and fierce. Nothing at all like I'd ever imagined I'd need, and yet the thought of life without him makes me want to cry.

I hardly know him, though.

And does he really know me?

He doesn't even know that I model, that I hold a master's degree in marketing, and he's never met any one of my friends.

But I don't want them to meet him.

My friends are high class, well-to-do, and respected members of society that would scorn a man who has his freaking wallet attached to his belt with a chain. They date clean-shaven men who wear custom-made suits from Italy and talk about the size of their diamond rings and yachts. None of them use the word "fuck" like it's a noun, verb, *and* adjective, and the thought of any of those guys with one tat, let alone two sleeves and tattooed knuckles, is actually amusing. The friends I know would stare in unabashed shock at Levi's thick beard and calloused hands.

Up until recently, that was me.

And now...

I shove the doubts out of my mind and take the book I picked up at the store today out of my bag. He told me to rest, and there's nowhere I'd rather be than right up here on his porch swing, with Murry curled up beside me, his little tail tapping the wooden stair. I can hear the water running in the kitchen while Levi loads the dishwasher. When the dishwasher begins whirring, the screen door squeaks and Levi stands in the doorway, barefoot, faded jeans slung low on his waist, his black t-shirt snug and form-fitting. My heart does a completely somersault.

"What'cha reading?" he asks. I go to sit up and but he gently pushes me back down, shifts me over so that he folds onto the seat and nestles his head in my lap. He looks at my book in my hand.

"It's historical romance," I say. "My favorite. I haven't read one in a few weeks, but this just came out." He raises a brow at the blonde woman in a pretty blue gown, standing in front of the setting sun, and reaches out a hand to take my book.

"Levi, don't," I say, waiting for him to tease me about it, but once he's got something on his mind, he doesn't even think twice. He plucks it out of my hand and fans it open.

"Daddy," I plead.

He cocks a thick brow at me and I stop protesting. "You're on chapter eight?" he asks, noting my bookmark. I nod.

"Relax," he says. I relax into him and close my eyes. It was a long a day. I was up early, worked hard, and now, sitting here on this porch swing with my head in his lap, I feel the tension seep out of my body. And then he reads. Damn, he knows how to read. His deep voice rises and falls with a natural cadence. He doesn't mock or tease but reads like I'm his little girl and this is my bedtime story. I smile, the setting sun basking me in warmth, and listen to him read.

I don't know I dozed off until I wake a while later when he lifts me up and cradles me against his chest. I sling my arms around his shoulders and he hushes me. "Shh, baby," he says. "Let's get you to bed." He strips me, lays me down in his huge bed, and tucks me in. No one's ever tucked me in before. My parents were standoffish and busy. This is nice. I sink under the covers and when he crawls in beside me, I fall into a deep, restful sleep.

I wake the next day with a start. Suddenly, I remember I had a job to do that I completely forgot about the day before. Levi's already up and in the shower. I knock on the door, stark naked but really needing to get in that shower.

"Daddy! I need to come in."

"Come in, then," he yells over the sound of the pounding water.

The bathroom off the master room is large and spacious and just slightly old-fashioned. The shower's huge to accommodate a guy like him, though. I don't want to smell like masculine soap all day, but I have to do my best. I don't have time to get to my place. And why would I think to bring my things to his place when we're only so short term?

"Can I come in?" I ask.

"If you don't, I'll spank your ass," he responds.

Well that got a good vibe skitting right down to my pussy. I tentatively pull back the curtain and step into the shower. Even though it's warm, I shiver when I see him large, muscled, naked body all lathered up with soap.

"Well good morning," I murmur. Suddenly my urgency to get in and out fades from my mind. I need to touch him.

I reach for the large bar of white soap he has in his hand and take it from him. He bends down, cups my face in his hand, and gives me a hot, heated, wet, good morning kiss. When he pulls away I soap up his back and chest, letting my hands roam along the hair on his chest, the muscles on his arms, and flat, hard planes of his chest. I look him in the eye when my hands roam further. His thick cock lengthens in my hand while I soap him up.

"Jesus," he groans. "Well good morning to you."

He's clean and so damn ready, I fall to my knees.

"May I, daddy?" I ask, as the warm stream of water hits my back and ass. The heat's so relaxing as it skates down my back. But the sight of him like this, our vulnerability naked and wet in the shower, has my body already teeming with a pulse of need. I lick my lips and swallow. I want his cock.

He fists my wet hair in his hand and leads my mouth to his full erection.

"Yeah, baby," he says. "Jesus fucking Christ, she asks permission," he mumbles to himself. I eagerly take him in my mouth, closing my eyes and moaning around the silk-sheathed steel of his cock. When he groans I feel arousal drip down my legs. I bob my head, needing so desperately to please him, to let him know how much this means to me, all of it. No one's ever taken care of me the way he does. No one's ever been so fierce and protective. He needs to be as happy as I am.

I suckle him hard, then draw the top of my tongue along the veins of his swollen cock. He groans and curses, then thrusts into my mouth. I brace myself by holding onto his strong, sturdy legs, taking him as he plunges into me. I can tell he's close by the way he tenses and the grip on my hair tightens. When he shoots into my mouth I swallow. I want every bit of him. I need this.

"Motherfucker," he moans, when I finally get to my feet in the shower. He pulls me to his chest. Steam rises between us. He holds me, his heartbeat thudding against my cheek. "God, baby. Jesus, *God*, baby, that was fucking amazing." He kisses the top of my hair. "Thank you."

"You're welcome," I reply, a warmth flooding my chest. "I like to please you, daddy. But I have to go."

"Go? Where?"

"I have a job to do," I say, not able to meet his eyes. "I told you my work was flexible, and it is, but sometimes things come up that need my attention."

I wonder if he's going to ask questions. Does he want

to know? Do I want him to ask questions, or is better if he doesn't? After a beat, he just says, "Okay, baby. But tonight, we'll have dinner wherever you want, and you give me details about this job you're doing."

That gives me a little time to think of how I want to approach this.

"Yes, daddy. So, do you have any neutral-smelling soap?"

He laughs, spins me around, and slaps my ass, which hurts like hell when my skin is all wet like this, but my pussy throbs with need. I don't have time, though.

"Got more than *neutral-smelling* soap," he mocks. He pushes the curtain aside and reveals a pale pink bottle of body wash and a light blue razor.

"For me?" I ask.

"Babe, I don't use pink body wash and I sure as fuck don't use a *razor*."

Giggling, I take the soap. "Well, thank you," I tell him. "That was thoughtful of you."

He doesn't reply but pulls me to his torso. He runs his hands along my breasts, takes the soap out of my hands and soaps me up. "I don't have time for this, daddy," I groan. "Oh, God, I wish I did."

"You sure, babygirl?" he asks, running his hands along my thighs. His thumb circles my clit with a gentle push that makes me jerk my pelvis. "Daddy has time for you if you can spare a few minutes." I want to. I *so* fucking want to. But I have to go, and I'm not sure I can really spare any extra time. Then he bends his head down, turns me to face him, and pulls my nipple into his mouth while he fingers my clit.

That does it. Fuck the time.

I throw my arms around his shoulder and my head lolls to the side. He strokes and fingers my pussy, lips and suckles my nipples, and soon I'm soaring into my release, my climax shattering me.

"Jesus, it's beautiful when you come," he says. "I could fuck you all over again. But you've gotta go." After we finish washing and my legs are shaved, he shuts off the water, steps out, and wraps himself in a towel. Next he helps me out, then wraps a huge, fluffy blue towel around me. He kneels, towel-drying me off.

"Is this what a daddy does?" I ask quietly.

He nods.

"I don't know much about daddy things. Like in a *relationship*," I stammer. "But I maybe googled a little."

He nods and continues to towel me off. "To tell you the truth, baby, I don't give a shit what other people do. I know there's shit like daddy doms at kink or sex clubs, and they can do whatever the fuck they want. That doesn't have to be what we do."

"This doesn't surprise me," I say with a giggle. He finishes toweling me, then hands me my bag of clothes. As I get dressed, he sits on the bed and watches me. I talk to him about what I read.

"So I guess daddies like to take care of their little girls," I say. "They have rules and consequences and discipline."

"Yeah?" He stands, reaching to his dresser and taking a pair of jeans and a t-shirt out of his drawer. "How do you feel about that?"

"I have no idea. I mean, we don't even have a safeword."

He scowls. "What the fuck's a safeword?" he asks. "Sounds like a waste of time to me."

I stifle a giggle. He's adorable when he gets all irritated.

"You say it when you don't want to do something," I try to explain, but already know it's a waste of time. Levi doesn't play by the rules. He doesn't do what he "should."

He does what he wants to. And hell, if I'm honest, it's kind of what I like about him.

"Your body tells me if you don't want to do something," he says. "And if I somehow miss that clue, babe, you tell me with your own words."

I know it's a little more complicated than that, but I don't want to waste my time telling him. What we have is maybe a little different than what others do, but it's what I like about it.

He comes up behind me, dressed in just his jeans, his bare torso pressed up against me as he wraps his arms around me. He smells clean and fresh, and I love the feel of his strong arm around me as he holds me. "There are things daddies can do," he says, "and things *this* daddy can do. I like the idea of having rules for you, but not just for the sake of having rules. I'll have them and I'll enforce them if it's how I can take care of you. It feels good and right with you." He nods against my hair and inhales deeply. "Rules and accountability and discipline? Yeah, baby. Daddy likes that."

I remember how he read to me last night, how he tucked me in. Today in the shower how he lathered me up and toweled me off.

I nod. I like this. Levi doesn't need anyone to tell him how to do things. He's a natural.

He bends down and kisses my cheek, then lets me go to finish getting ready. I wonder what he'll have in mind. Levi is Levi. He'll growl, "get the hell to bed" when I'm tired and expect me to do what he says. I don't see anything formal or structured in our future, though.

Do we have a future?

It makes me feel warm and tingly inside, though. I like that. I like it a lot.

But my phone buzzes and I'm distracted, trying to pull

on clothes and towel dry and talk to Levi all at once, so I don't look at who's on the line.

Damn, it's my agent.

"I have to take this," I tell him. I feel a little guilty not telling him who's calling after the intimacy we've shared. He has no idea what I do. "Let's talk later?"

He fastens his belt and nods. "Later."

I scurry out to the kitchen and walk to the porch. My car's still on the street. It feels weird holding things back from him, even though I really have only known him for a few days. I'm even a little disappointed he doesn't push ask more questions. Does he care? I have no idea what I want from him myself.

"Hello?" I ask, sliding into the driver's seat. I haven't even done my hair or makeup but it doesn't matter, since they'll fix all that at the studio.

"Tanya, where have you *been?* Girl, we got a proposition you would not believe." Blaise, my agent, chatters on and on and I'm only half-listening because honestly I get "propositions I would not believe" on a fairly regular basis. But at the word *classic car* I almost crash the car.

"Say that again, Blaise?"

"Baby, this magazine is the best of the best. And you wouldn't believe the money they're offering." He tells me my advance I feel my jaw go slack.

"What do they want?" I ask.

He lays out the job, and it's not that different from other ones I've done.

"Only one condition, Tanya."

I sigh. He's led me on, told me the offer, and now he's giving me the rest of the story.

"Yeah?"

"Full face this time."

I do hand photo shoots, body photo shoots, back and

ass shots even but I do not put my face in a modeling shoot. It's a point of pride and my niche.

"Think about it, Tanya. You're *beautiful,* and I think this would work well for you."

The problem is, this is something that might end up under Levi's eyes, and I can't stand the thought.

"No," I tell Blaise, cringing. It's the biggest job offer I got this year, and I'm crazy to turn it down. And why do I care what Levi thinks? He's my boss-with-benefits.

"Are you crazy?" he asks. "You haven't gotten an offer like this in so long, Tanya, and I have to remind you, as your very honest and upfront agent, that you aren't getting any younger."

I grit my teeth together so I don't say something I regret. And honestly, when I do a job like this it's easily four to six months before the pictures even hit the press and by then...my stomach drops and my throat gets all clogged. By then it won't matter what Levi thinks because I'll be long gone. Still, I don't like the idea of him seeing me in a magazine or something. I flush when I think that *even if* they only did a body shoot, he might know it was me.

I hang up the phone after giving Blaise some excuse about things to do and a poor connection, and drive toward the shop. I grab a cup of coffee at a drive through, and the entire time I'm thinking about what to do. I can't really afford to be turning down too many offers, and Blaise is right. I'm *not* getting any younger. This is a seasonal job and won't always pay the bills, but hell if I'll work for my father.

I shove all my worries away. I don't have time to think about this now. With a sigh, I circle around looking for a parking spot and finally find one in the back on the street. It's a little ways away from the entrance, but close enough.

I shut my car door and see Grease and Spade standing near a pile of tools they're cleaning.

"Told Levi I'd keep it a secret," he says. My ears perk up but I keep walking. I shouldn't eavesdrop. This is a stupid choice, and yet I can't help myself. "But dude, gotta tell someone." The way he talks, he's about to divulge something really juicy. What a douchebag. He sounds like a high school girl.

"Yeah?" Grease says, rubbing a rag on a tool. "You think Levi's cool with that? Don't be an asswipe."

Good man, Grease. He likes the muffins I brought in the other day. I make a mental note to bring them in again.

"Dude, I was talking to Mandy, though."

Mandy, Mandy…where do I know that name? Oh! The blonde Barbie from the other day. I freeze behind a bush with my coffee suspended in mid-air. It's scalding my hand and I'm switching it from one to the next, but I need to hear this. Spade leans over and says, "She's pregnant, man. And she knows *exactly* who the father is."

"No shit," Grease mutters. "Levi?"

Despite my scalding hand, my body goes numb and cold when Spade confirms this suspicion. It doesn't matter. It doesn't fucking *matter* I tell myself. He's nothing to me. He's *less* than nothing to me. He's a guy I slept with, and he's fixing my father's car. That's it.

I'm here to get this done, then I am so out of here.

On impulse, I pick up my phone and call Blaise back.

"Offer still on the table?" I ask. "I'm considering it. Not decided yet, but maybe…"

I can practically hear him clapping his hands in glee.

Chapter Ten

Levi

Jesus, the girl's got my head so in the clouds, I'm a full thirty minutes late to work. I walked the dogs and got them set for the day, then head into the office. It sucks that she's not here that much longer. Walking into the shop with Tanya no longer there seems dismal. I love the way her face lights up when I walk in. And hell, the place looks so much better now that she's here.

It isn't just her at the shop I'll miss, though. It's just... her. This morning, the way she just *gave* herself to me like that. And last night, the way she fell asleep when I was reading that book to her, all little-girl like with her hair tousled in the wind and her arm across her chest, she's doing things to me I can't help control. I like taking care of her. It feels natural and right.

I want more of her. My thoughts are running to all things Tanya.

So when I come into the shop and she shoots me a frosty glare, I'm taken aback. What the hell is this?

"Hey, baby," I say, coming up to her and kissing her cheek.

But she pulls away.

What the fuck is that about?

"Tanya," I warn. I don't know why she's giving me the cold shoulder. We were good this morning. But the door to the shop opens and Spade walks in.

"Morning, boss," he says. He nods and shoots Tanya a wink. "Tanya."

Heat curls in my gut. I don't like him fucking winking at her.

"Morning," I grit out. "How's that paint job coming? And did you get the parts for the Corvette?"

We talk about the various jobs we're working on, then he leaves.

"How's my father's car coming?" Tanya asks me, not meeting my eyes. The phone rings just as I answer, and she picks it up, turning her back to me. I frown, watching her. Someone's gonna get her little ass spanked if she thinks the she can go all frigid on me without recourse. When she's done taking the message, she hangs up the receiver. I push it away from her, then swivel her chair around to face me. I stand on either side of her legs, caging her in. "Tanya," I say. "What the fuck is going on? Spill, babe."

"It's nothing," she says with a toss of her head.

I lean in. "It's not *nothing*," I say to her. "And if you don't tell me why you're behaving this way, I'm gonna pick you up, take you to my truck, pull that skirt of yours up and spank the truth right outta you."

She crosses her arms on her chest and shoots me a venomous look. "Maybe you should tell *me, daddy.*" She narrows her eyes when she says daddy like that's some sorta clue, but I'm baffled.

We can't talk, though, because the door to the shop

opens again and Grease comes in with something that needs my attention right away.

"Conversation's not over, Tanya," I tell her. Grease shoots me a sympathetic look, but guys don't talk about relationship shit, so he says nothing. I answer his question, and when I go back to the main office, Tanya's gone.

Chapter Eleven

Tanya

I SHOULD MAYBE GIVE Levi a chance. But honest to God, I hardly know the guy. I'm so mad at myself for falling for a guy like him anyway. I need him to do work no one else could, and I allowed him to manipulate me like a fool.

Of *course* he got a girl pregnant. What makes me think I'm so special? I could cry. Hell, I think I might. So when he goes back in the shop, I decide I'm going for a little walk. It'll piss him off when he finds out I left, but I don't care. Maybe I want to piss him off. I take my bag and leave, head out the front door, and let it shut behind me. I know I'm being childish, but I'm more angry at myself than I am at him. I never should have let myself fall for a guy like Levi.

I'm hurt, really. And I feel entitled to take a little time to nurse my wounds.

He hasn't even done anything, really. So things got hot and heavy there for a bit. Soon, the car will be finished, and I'll never have to see him again. I have nothing to offer him. To a man like Levi, I'm likely shallow and superficial. I've got more money than I know what to do with and things that are important to me probably seem stupid to him.

But I've got to have something. Something to look forward to. Something that makes me happy. And maybe I like the thrill of a photo shoot. Maybe I enjoy the luxurious things in life I've worked hard for.

As I walk down the street alone, though, I wonder. How satisfying are these things if I have no one to share my life with? My hopes, and my dreams? And even more, my fears and struggles?

I walk and I walk and I walk. I don't know how long. I have no idea where.

My phone rings. If it's Levi, I am *not* answering it. I lift it and see *Jacked Up* on the screen. I silence the phone and walk a little faster. Maybe he'll wonder where I went.

Good.

My phone rings again, and I snatch it out of my purse, ready to tell Levi to go shove it. I answer it and huff into the phone, "*What?*"

"Tanya?"

It's Blaise.

"Oh, hi Blaise. Sorry about that," I mutter. I look around me and realize I have no idea where I am. I walked off in such a huff, I'm in some sort of neighborhood I've never seen before, and it doesn't look very nice. Definitely not a place where a girl wearing Prada should be walking.

I swallow hard and feel my skin prickle when a guy lighting up a smoke in a wrought-iron stairwell gives me a lewd once-over.

"Tanya, I just got the best news ever," Blaise says.

"Oh yeah?"

"Yes," he continues. "They've doubled their offer."

"Doubled?" He continues to tell me the rules and conditions. I squirm a little, but I have to admit I like the idea of Levi finding out a did a full front nude photo shoot for a car magazine. That'll serve him right.

"I'll do it," I breathe.

"Only thing is, they need you to do it *soon.*"

"How soon?"

"They're ready when you are."

I take in a deep breath, let it out slowly, and nod. "I'll do it today."

I get the address from him and shove it in my bag, then look around me wildly. I've just made a crazy, spur-of-the-moment decision, but I have no regrets.

Do I?

Only damn problem is, I have no idea where I am. I look around me and try to see back where I walked to, but my head was so in the clouds I don't have a clue. There's a cluster of guys over by a convenience store sharing a joint. The sweet, acrid smell churns my stomach a little. I need to get out of here.

Flashing my most winsome smile, I approach them. "Boys? Can someone help me?"

A tall, muscular guy who's easily ten years my junior steps in the front.

"Well hello there," he says, making the rest of them snicker.

"I seem to have lost my way," I tell him. Hopefully I can charm him. "Do you know how to get back to…" I almost tell him my address, but that feels wrong. I could tell him Levi's, but that's also just not smart. "Jacked Up?" I finish.

"Classic car shop?" he asks.

They mutter among themselves and I hear the name

Levi DeRocco. One guy shakes his head and another's eyes go wide.

"You his girl?" the blond asks, his jaw hardening. And then I realize, they don't want to come near me if I'm his. Seems his reputation has preceded me.

I swallow. Am I?

"No," I say, not sure if it's the truth or a lie. "But I work there." Or did?

I just need to get out of here.

"I'll take you," blondie says.

"I'll pay you," I tell him.

He shoots me a lewd grin. "That you will."

The rest of them hoot and holler, and my blood runs cold. What do I do now? But whatever. I have to get out of here.

He takes my hand and leads me down the street, the sounds of the others fading, and thankfully when we get to a small, beat-up car in front of a fire hydrant, he lets go of my arm and the façade fades. "I'll take you back," he says. "I want to know the truth, though." He's sober now, with none of the swagger he had in front of the others. Seems he was putting on a front for them. I breathe out a sigh of relief. He asks me with a look of concern, "Are you Levi's?"

I shift uncomfortably. "I was," I tell him, looking down.

He nods. "Fair enough. I'm not gonna touch you, and I don't want your money. I *do* want to go home tonight with all my teeth and my nuts in place, though. Got it?"

I give him a watery smile. "Yeah," I say. "Got it." I get in the passenger side door, and it's thankfully clean in here. In silence, we drive out of this little neighborhood, and after a few minutes, things begin to look familiar again.

"Here," I tell him, when we're right near Jacked Up. "Um, maybe drop me here."

"Jesus Christ," the kid mutters. "Knew you were his."

"I'm not," I say, but he only gives me a sidelong glance.

He purses his lips and rolls his eyes. "Look, lady, I don't really give a shit if you got into a little *spat* with Levi or whatever. You'll kiss and make up and live happily ever after, but you and I never met, yeah?"

I nod. "Yeah," I say. "And thank you."

He's young, and a little tough around the edges, but he seems genuine enough.

"Um, do you have any idea how to get to…" my voice trails off as I take out my phone and read the address.

He looks, reads the address, and nods. "GPS directions there are shit. Take the main road here until you get to the Five Corners intersection, then go *over* the bridge. After that, directions will pan out."

I smile at him gratefully, then take a wad of cash out of my wallet, drop it on the seat, then leave before he can respond. I get out of the car, and head to the shop, the sound of his car accelerating fading into the distance.

I get to my car, but as I open the door, my phone rings again. The skin prickles on my neck, as if someone's watching me. I look around me, see no one, and ignore the phone ringing.

I pull out the address Blaise gave me. I have a job to do.

Chapter Twelve

Levii

I DON'T KNOW where that little brat went to, but when I get my hands on her she won't sit for a goddamned week.

The truck is shit for looking for someone, so loud and cumbersome, but I give it my best shot. It rumbles like a motherfucker and takes corners like a fucking elephant. Still, I've got nothing. I come back to the shop around lunchtime, and she's not there.

What the hell? This morning, things were great.

Maybe she isn't who I thought she was. It's only been a few days, but I thought I had a pretty good read on her. I thought we had a good thing going. I'm into her, more than I've ever been into anyone, and just this morning she started asking what it meant to be my babygirl.

And if this babygirl thinks she can go around flouncing away when she's upset about something, the first *rule* she'll learn is that I do not appreciate childish behavior like that.

But hell, we didn't even fight. So I'm kinda bewildered.

I have shit to do, though, including finishing the job on her father's car, so I go back to the shop. The phone rings off the wall, there are more customers coming into the shop thanin the last week, and I can't find the coffee filters. Minor details, but it all pisses me off.

Finally, by late afternoon, I'm starving and getting more pissed off by the minute, so I leave the job I'm doing, clean up, and figure I'll get something to eat. The others have all left the shop, but Spade's entering order details on the computer in the office.

"Have you seen Tanya today, man?" I ask.

Clicking away on the computer, he doesn't look at me when he answers. "Saw her pull up a little while ago with some blond guy in a beat-up Ford," he says. "No idea who that was, but she leaned over and gave him something. Didn't see what they did, but she did kiss him. Then she got out, got into her car, and took off."

Some blond guy? *Kissed* him? What the fuck is that about?

I don't trust him. I need to lose this asshole.

I growl to myself. I don't want him knowing I'm pissed at her but Jesus *fucking* Christ, I'm pissed at her. And I'm not giving up, either. There's something special about Tanya.

She wants rules and discipline? She'll get rules and discipline.

I call her one more time, knowing that she isn't going to pick up the phone. Spade says he saw a guy drop her off outside the shop, though. I can do a little investigative work. The security cameras run outside the shop since we have inventory that's worth a shit ton of money. I don't have a need to look at them often, but I can when I need to. I go to the small room inside the shop where the security footage rolls by on camera, and it's an easy matter to scroll back through the last couple of hours. I go a little further back than I mean to, though, all the way to this morning. Spade and Grease are in the back, and I can see the side profile of Tanya behind a bush behind them. I scowl at the screen when I see what happens. The two of them are talking. She goes rigid, shakes her head, and backs up, then turns tail and runs away.

On the second screen I see her walking to the front of the shop. Her head's in her hands and she looks distraught. Jesus. My fists clench by my side. What did she hear them say? Where is she now? Is this my clue to what's going on? Anger flares in my gut. I have to play a fucking detective to find out what's going on?

I fast forward on the security footage and see her leave the shop, then keep scrolling until I see what Spade was talking about. *Christ* almighty, he's right. She's in the car of some blond kid. She doesn't lean over and kiss him like he said, but takes what looks like a bunch of cash out of her purse, tosses it on the seat, then leaves. He lifts it up and yells to her, but she takes off.

Why would Spade lie about that? Did he think he saw them kiss?

I zone in on the plate, jot it down, and look it up. We've got a detailed database of this shit because we're always looking for parts and pieces, and even though it may not be strictly legal, I don't give a damn. I get the address registered to that plate, get in my truck, dial her one more time until it gets to voicemail, and take off.

Spade and I need to have a chat, too, but blondie's more pressing.

When I pull up to the seedy apartment complex I found listed, there's got to be a dozen guys sitting around on the stoop. When they see my truck they scatter like mice, except for one. Blondie.

Smart kid.

I shut the door of my truck, stalk over to him, and the kid stands his ground. Gotta respect that. I may not need to beat the truth out of him after all.

"You know who I am?" I ask him. I grew up in this neighborhood. Fucking everyone knows who I am.

He nods and swallows, his Adam's apple bobbing up and down.

"Swear to God I didn't touch her," he says, lifting his head up and meeting my eyes.

Gotta respect a brother for that.

"Good," I tell him. "Never met you but I don't much like hurting guys I just met. So just tell me the truth and we're good."

He shrugs, but his eyes betray his fear. "She asked for a ride. Got here by accident, needed a ride. Gotta tell you, man, I asked her repeatedly if she was yours. Told her I wanted nothing to do with her if she was."

That surprises me. "Yeah?"

He nods. "She told me she wasn't. And anyway, man, swear to God, all I did was give her a ride." He shrugs and looks a bit bashful. "Girl like her really shouldn't be around these parts anyway."

He's got that right. "You took her back to the shop," I say.

He nods.

"Any idea where she went after that?"

His eyes brighten and he looks hopeful, probably convinced that getting into my good favor is in his best interest. He's not wrong.

"Yeah, she asked me how to get to the Corner District," he says. "I told her GPS gets confusing and gave her directions to get there safely."

I feel like clouds have just parted on a sunny day, and I'm basking in a beam of sunlight.

"Excellent," I tell him, reaching out to give him a fist bump. He bumps my fist and smiles.

"Um, she gave me some money," he says, taking a large roll of bills out of his pocket. "It's way too much." He goes to hand it to me.

"Keep it, kid," I tell him. "And thank you."

I get back in my truck and head to the District. I have no idea where she is or what she's doing, but I'll find her. And when I do, she'll have a few things to answer for.

Chapter Thirteen

Tanya

This feels wrong. It didn't used to. I used to love stripping down and posing for the camera. I felt like a goddess with my body on display. Now, after stripping for Levi, and feeling his hands all over my body… now, it doesn't feel right anymore.

We take over ninety shots before I'm so hungry and thirsty I need something, but Blaise frowns when I suggest a break.

"No eating and drinking on a shoot," he says, dismissing me with a wave of his hand. Blaise is short and balding, with gray hair and circular glasses perched high on his nose. He's the best agent in the industry but can be a slave driver during a shoot.

The photographer shoots me a sympathetic smile. "Fifty more, *cherie*, and we are done," he says in a thick French accent.

I swallow and nod with a sigh. The photographer hands me a silk scarf. "Tie that around your neck and let the ends dangle right above your breasts," he says.

Jacked Up

I nod. We're in a dark room with drawn black velvet curtains. There's some furniture and props, and the makeup artist sits by the door. She leaps to her feet when there's a loud commotion outside the door.

I blink when the door swings open and look wildly around to cover myself up with something, but all I've got is this silk. My jaw drops when Levi storms into the room.

Holy *shit*. He looks like he could murder someone with his bare hands.

But God. He's beautiful, like an avenging angel with light shining around him. And when I look at him, my heart sinks to my toes. I fucked up. I fucked up bad. And he's pissed off, but he has a right to be. When his eyes meet mine, I feel the truth down to my bones.

Everything I thought was a lie.

Spade played me for a fool. But more importantly, I *do* mean something to him. This man came to find me. He came for me.

"Get out of here!" Blaise shouts, but Levi shoots him a glare so withering Blaise slinks into the corner like a scolded puppy. The photographer steps back from his camera, and just in time, too, because Levi crosses the room, picks it up in his massive hands, and literally smashes the thing.

"Not your fault," he says to the photographer. "But *no one* looks at my girl dressed like *that* and lives to tell about it. Consider this your warning." The photographer looks around the room wildly, but Levi's already moved on.

"They're already uploaded to the cloud!" Blaise stammers from the corner, but Levi swings his gaze to his with enough heat to melt an iceberg.

"They *were* uploaded to the cloud," he says. "Already talked to the owner out front and wrote a check so that I now personally own every one of those goddamned photos." He looks at the photographer. "And you can bill me for the equipment. No hard feelings?"

The photographer just blinks at Levi's large, tattooed, seriously furious body and nods. He says something incoherent that sounds like "Ungh." Then Levi turns to me.

I was angry at him. Now I'm a little scared and sad and I feel like I'm going to cry. He crosses the room to me in three long strides.

"And *you*, little girl," he says. He tugs the end of the scarf I'm still wearing and pulls me to him, lifts me into the air, and tosses me over his shoulder like I weigh nothing at all, "will come with me." He stalks out of the room. When we get to the mercifully vacant changing room, he places me down on my feet, locates my pile of clothes, then dresses me himself without speaking a word. I can feel the anger radiating off him in waves. I don't know what to say at first, so I say nothing. It isn't until he slips my second shoe on that I finally find my tongue.

"How'd you find me?" I ask. His lips are thinned and his eyes dangerously heated. He doesn't respond, so I don't repeat my question.

He takes me by the elbow and frog-marches me out of the studio. My cheeks flame with embarrassment but given what he just did to the photographer's equipment, I'm probably lucky he isn't taking me right across his lap in the waiting room.

And a little part of me is happy that…he came for me. He may be angry right now, but he came for me.

He lifts me straight into his truck, even buckles me in, all in silence. I shiver. I'm in so much damn trouble. But God, I deserve it.

We drive in silence for a few blocks when finally I can't help it. "I overheard something this morning," I tell him. "It wasn't true, was it?"

Jacked Up

He turns and fixes me with a scorching stare. "Depends, princess. I don't know what you heard. Maybe if I did, you'd give me a chance to tell you the truth."

I swallow. Ouch. "Spade said you knocked up Barbie," I say, her name momentarily escaping me.

He blinks. "Say *what?*"

"The blonde girl," I stammer. "The woman who came into the office my first day. She's pregnant, and Spade told Grease you were the daddy."

"What is this, goddamned motherfucking seventh grade?" he asks, a vein pulsing in his neck.

Oh boy. Yeah, I'm toast.

"Um," is all I can say.

He continues in a barely-coherent growl. "First, I never even so much as kissed that frigid bitch. Second, even if I *did*, I wouldn't be stupid enough to knock her up. Third, and this is a big third, you ever have a question about something like that, you fucking *ask* me." He shakes his head. "Jesus fucking Christ," he curses. "I am not the kinda guy that hides shit."

Of course he isn't. God, I was dumb.

"You couldn't even ask me?" he continues. "Just stormed off like a fucking toddler?"

Tears prick my eyes. He's right.

"I should've spanked it out of you this morning like I threatened to," he says.

"How'd you find me?" I ask. I need to apologize, but not yet.

"I went back through security footage, saw you getting dropped off with the blond kid, found him, asked questions."

Oh *no.*

"Did you hurt him?" I ask him.

He gives me a sidelong glare. "Do I need to?"

My heart thumps madly. He would.

"No," I stammer. "I—no."

"The only one getting hurt around here is *you*," he says, "Once I calm the hell down. You asked for rules, princess. You wanted discipline."

Oh, right. I have the worst damn timing.

"But Spade and I are gonna have words, too." Good. The total douchebag. I hope he kicks his ass. And then I realize he's driving toward the shop, not toward his house like I suspected. "I'd rather deal with *him* when I'm pissed, and you once I've calmed down."

Ever the gentleman, I guess.

He pulls up outside the shop. Turning to me, he points a finger in my direction. "You stay *right there*."

After my dumb move this morning, I'm doing exactly what he says. I'm curious, though, so I roll down my window. He didn't say anything about the window.

Levi storms into the shop. There are a few people at the counter. He speaks to each one of them, hands one some paperwork to fill out, reaches for the phone and hits a few buttons. I feel a little guilty. I should be the one in there helping him. Seriously, though, I'm not so stupid I'm going to disobey him. Not now. Not after this morning.

After the people in the front room are gone, he moves into the back. I don't hear anything, and I'm waiting. Behind the shop, I hear an engine roaring to life, and I peer out the window. It's Spade, and he's taking off. The dude is up to no good and I wonder what the hell is going on.

I want to jump out and get Levi, but I can't. I don't have to wait long, though. A few minutes later, Levi storms out to the truck.

"Spade's gone," he says.

"I know. I saw him drive off," I tell him.

He shakes his head and starts his truck. "I'm taking you back to your place," he says. "You're going to pack a bag. After today, I don't want to let you out of my sight."

I nod quietly. This. This is what I want. This is what I *need*. So I say the only thing I can. The only thing that's *right*.

"Yes, daddy."

He reaches for my knee and surprises me by giving me a gentle squeeze.

"That's my girl."

I know I'm going to end up over his lap, and soon, and there's a part of me that's scared and a part of that's mildly turned on. He's all raw alpha male. But I can't help thinking about one thing that plays over and over in my mind.

He came for me. He razed the damn path to find me and got me. And I don't even care what's going to happen to my career, or those photos.

Then I remember what he said, as if I've suppressed it from my memory until now.

"Daddy?"

"Mm?"

"You said you…bought the photos?" I know what they were going to pay me for those.

"Yeah," he says quietly. "But Tanya, I wouldn't bring this up right now if I were you."

That sends a tingle right down my spine. So I close my mouth when we drive to my place. He parks his truck in the lot, comes around and helps me out, and we walk silently to my apartment. It feels weird being here now. I was so proud of this place. But now, the gleaming chandelier and plush carpets, framed prints in the halls and light jazz music being piped through speakers on the elevator, pale in comparison to *his* place.

I want to feel those hardwood floors beneath my feet. I want to lie on his porch swing with Murry keeping silent vigil by the stairs, the sun setting and the wind rustling the pages of my book with my head in Levi's lap. I don't want this luxury anymore.

Luxury is being with him, apart from the hustle and bustle of the city. I want to bake cookies in that kitchen and serve lemonade in frosted glasses. I want to see snow fall on that porch and a fire roaring in the hearth. I want to fall asleep beside him, in his bed.

Sex with Levi is epic. Companionship with Levi is even better.

I open the door to my apartment, and he goes ahead of me. He takes me by the hand and leads me to my room. "I'm sorry, Levi," I whisper. "Daddy, I'm sorry."

"I know, baby," he says. Thankfully, it seems like his anger has abated a little. Even so, when he points to my bed, my heart does a little somersault. He may have calmed down, but those eyes bore right through me.

"Strip," he commands.

I swallow hard, my eyes trained on him as I slowly take off my clothes. My hands shake when my bra falls to the floor and I stand in front of him naked. He shrugs out of the leather jacket he wears and slides it onto a chair, eyes never leaving mine. He stands in front of me in his signature tight t-shirt, all strength and power somehow softened with his utter attention and focus. My eyes drop to his tattoos, but a firm, "eyes on me," gets my attention. There's a palpable difference in power here with me standing naked before him and him fully dressed.

But I like it.

He stalks to the bed, sits on the edge, and points silently to his knee with a frown that brooks no argument. I'm shaking a little, nervous and excited and aroused all at once, my mind a confused jumble of incoherent thoughts. We don't say anything. I can't even if I wanted to, and he doesn't need to.

We aren't going to fight. There will be no cold shoulder or silent treatment or angry words hurled at one another that will sting and mar. He's going to put peace between us right here, right now.

Gingerly, I lay myself over his lap and without a word, he captures both my wrists in his large hand, his rough, calloused palm gently scraping the tender skin. Pinning them to my back, he lifts his other hand, then slaps his palm against my ass. It stings and I buck, but he holds me tight. He spanks me hard and fast, but it's what I want. It's what I need. I feel like a total jerk for what I did, and I want to pay for it. Somehow, I have no idea how or why, when he does this, he cleanses me.

I lose track of how many times his palm raises and falls, but my skin's on fire, every inch of my backside throbbing and aching. And yet, I need more. I find myself sinking into this, submerged in nothing but me and daddy and my punishment. I'm yelping and sniffling. He isn't even harsh or exacting, but more matter-of-fact. I screwed up. We'll make this right. We'll do it with me over his knee. I'm crying and I don't know when I started or even why I'm crying, but it feels like the right thing to do. And here, over his lap, exposed and vulnerable and remorseful, I give in to tears.

I don't know how long I'm over his lap or when he stops, but I know at one point it's over, and he's lifting me up. He kisses me, a brief touch, soft and intimate, over my salty lips. I taste the tears and Levi, all stern and masculine and protective. Somewhere deep inside I want more. I need to feel him, connect again in the deepest, most intimate way possible. It's not even the physical need so much as a deeper, more emotional craving.

I was a spoiled little girl, and now he gives me what I didn't even know I needed.

When did this happen? I can't think anymore, though, because now he's lifting me up and laying me on my back. Most of the time, he fucks me hard and from behind, fisting my hair or slapping my ass while he takes me. But this time, he kneels over me, his eyes never leaving mine.

I love you, I think, but that can't be possible, not so soon. I don't believe in instalove. Well, I didn't. I swallow what I want to say and open my arms for him to draw closer. Once he's stripped, he slowly lowers himself to me. His mouth comes to mine, and with purposeful, deliberate strokes, he makes me his again.

Chapter Fourteen

Levi

I HOLD her on my bare chest. Her long, long hair is strewn all around us, a pool of fragrant, golden brown beauty. She rises and falls on my chest when I inhale and exhale. I smooth my hand on her hair and think about the day we've had. When I woke up this morning, I had no idea what would happen. I didn't know she'd be so susceptible to lies like that, that she'd react so strongly. But she needs to know she can trust me, and this is just one way we'll bridge that trust. She won't run from me. She won't hide from me.

I'm not angry at her anymore, but I hope she's learned her lesson.

"Tanya?" I'm not sure if she's awake or asleep.

"Mmm?"

I stroke her hair, and my arms tighten around her. "If you ever have a question about something, what will you do?"

She takes a deep breath in. I watch her bare shoulders rise and then fall. "Talk to you, daddy." I bend down and kiss the top of her head.

"Good girl."

We lay there for a little while longer, until I hear her stomach growl. "Hungry, baby?"

"Starving."

"Have you had anything to eat today?"

She sighs. "I don't even remember."

"Okay, well first thing we do is get something to eat," I say.

She pushes up so her chin is in her hand while she looks at me. "I had chicken marinating in the fridge at your place," she says wistfully. "Probably should cook that."

"You want to go to my place?"

Her eyes get a little wide and she nods, biting her lip. "Yes, daddy." Looking around her huge, well-furnished bedroom, she shrugs a little. "You know, I kinda like your place better than mine. No, I *definitely* do."

I huff out a laugh. "Good, because I definitely like my place better than yours, too."

She snorts, rolls over, and starts looking around for her clothes. I get up and do the same. I'm buttoning my jeans when she turns to me, dressed now, running her fingers through her long hair. "Levi?"

"Yeah, baby?" I say, pulling my t-shirt on. She reaches her hand out to my arm to get my attention. Her eyes warm and she smiles.

"Thank you."

I'm not sure what she's even thanking me for, but I just give her a kiss and tell her, "You're welcome, baby."

Jacked Up

THE SUN'S setting when we head to my place. It's a little bit of a drive, but not too bad.

"The dogs will be ready to go out when we get back," I say. "I'll take them out and you want to start dinner? Or do you want me to fire up the grill?"

"Would you mind if I take them out?" she asks. "I'm dying to get some fresh air, and I think the grill would be perfect."

"No problem."

I park my truck on the curb, come around and help her out. The dogs run at us when we come, and she bends down, greeting them with a smile. I hand her the leashes from the hook inside the door, she snaps them on, and goes down the stairs. Shrugging out of my jacket, I walk to the kitchen to get the food ready, when a high-pitch scream fills the air.

Tanya.

I'm at a run before I even know what I'm doing.

She's not far, though, just in the side yard. I race to her. Her hand's over her mouth and she's pointing a shaking finger at the barn.

The doors swing crazily open, letting in sunlight that easily streams through the very vacant barn. Sal's '55 Jaguar is gone.

WE SIT in silence while police inspect the barn and ask us a million questions. I have no idea what the fuck is going on or who was here.

"Were you in the house at the time of the theft?"

I shake my head. "No. We just got home."

The young officer with short brown hair that sticks up a little in the back, nods.

"I see. And did you have insurance on the vehicle, sir?"

"Of course I did."

He raises a brow. 'May I ask your total of your insurance policy?"

Is he fucking kidding me? "Do you think I fabricated all this for a payout?" I ask.

The officer bristles.

"Levi," Tanya says, putting her hand on me.

I take in a deep breath and nod. For Christ's sake. I just want them to find the thief already. This is personal, and it also means I'm fucked at the show if we don't recover this.

I give him the info he needs, then go back to her. We sit on the porch swing, but tonight's not relaxing like it normally is. The dogs walk around, wagging their tails nervously at the officers combing our home. They don't know what to make of all of this. Hell, neither do I.

"Who would do this?" I mutter to myself, rubbing my hand across my face, when Tanya sits up straight.

"I know who'd do this," she says. She shakes her head, but a faint red flushes her cheeks. "I know *exactly* who would do this."

I give her a curious look.

"Who was the one who planted the idea of you getting someone pregnant?" she asks, her eyes boring into me.

"Spade," I say, my hands fisting. I'll beat the shit out of him.

She nods. "And who was the one who sent you looking for me? Told you how to find me?" she asks.

I nod. "Yeah."

"It was a diversion," she says, shaking her head and groaning. "He set us up, Levi."

I get to my feet and start to pace. "Goddamn it, of course it was. You know, when he told me he saw the blond kid drop you off, he told me he saw you kiss. What an *asshole*. I didn't think much of it when I went through the footage and found you hadn't. I assumed he just couldn't see jack from where he was, and he was seeing things."

She shakes her head. "I never even got close enough to kiss him. He just made that up to make you mad."

I nod.

"Levi?"

"Yeah?"

"Does it make you mad?" She's looking at me coyly, one leg tucked under her as she bites her lip.

I scowl at her with a noise that's half-growl. "You need another spanking, little girl, you keep up this line of conversation."

She grins at me. She likes that I'm jealous.

Well fuck me.

"Good news is, it's broad daylight," the officer says, coming up onto the porch. "Hard not to spot a car like that unless there's a good way to hide it. Did it drive still?"

"Like a goddamn dream," I say.

The officer nods curtly. "Then how would a full-sized classic car like that avoid suspicion?"

"Auto trailer would be the easiest, most efficient way," I tell him. "There are a couple of ways it can be done, but that's by far the easiest."

"So we send out notifications to be on the lookout for an auto trailer," the officer says. "Done." He picks up his phone and steps to the side to make a call.

"It hasn't been gone that long," I tell him. He nods, then starts talking on the phone.

Tanya holds my hand.

"It's just a car," I tell her.

She squeezes.

"No, daddy," she says softly so the others can't hear. "It's more than that, and you know it is."

This girl gets me. I swallow hard and nod. "Yeah," I say gruffly. "It is."

It represents a friendship I had when I was just becoming a man. Years of hard work. Dreams and visions and goals. And the idea of someone taking it…

"Let's go," she says. "Let's go and look for it. Just me and you."

Just go? She wants to get in the car with me and drive and find my car. Drop everything and just *go*.

I give her a long look while I mull over our options. We've got the police combing the area for the car, and she thinks we'll find it on our own?

"Eat," I tell her. "You've got to eat."

She gets up, walks to the kitchen, and opens the cabinet. She tears open a box of granola bars that I didn't even know I had, grabs four of them, then says, "Let's *go*."

Damn, this girl is gonna keep me on my toes. Which is exactly what I love about her.

I take her by the hand, and we go.

Chapter Fifteen

Tanya

I HAVE no idea where to go or how I'll help Levi find his car, but when we do find it, I'm going to slap Spade silly. Or maybe I'll knee him in the nuts. The son of a bitch set us up, made sure we were distracted today, and then did this. I know it was him. I never did like the jerk.

"Think," I tell Levi. "Let's think. Where would he be going with this? What would he gain from this?"

Levi huffs out a mirthless laugh. "Besides millions of dollars?"

"Well, I mean, where would he be able to get that money most easily?" I ask.

He tugs at his beard. "That's a good question. I have no idea."

Suddenly, a crazy idea comes to me, and I have to tell him. "Wait. Levi. You said that you found me by running through the footage in your office, right? The cameras?"

He nods. "Yep."

"Well, what was Spade doing at the time? If this was him, and he was planning on getting you out of the office, he was just biding his time until you left, right?"

"Right. He was on the computer," I tell her. "I thought he was getting specs for a car we were working on in the database."

I nod. "Well…maybe he wasn't, though. It can't hurt to go back to the shop and look at the footage of the cameras in the *office*. What if he did something that would give us a clue?"

He leans over, smiles at me, and plants a kiss on my forehead. "You're adorable, you know that? All detective-like."

I smile shyly. I like earning his approval. I think with any other guy I'd find this condescending, but not with Levi. "Thank you," I say. "Now let's *go*." He gives me an affectionate slap on the ass.

"Watch it, sweetheart," he says in my ear. "Daddy's still the one in charge." And damn if that doesn't make me melt.

He tells the officers we're going to look at a few things and they tell us they'll call us if anything comes up. So far, there are no leads, though. No one's seen a car-transport trailer anywhere in the nearby vicinity.

We head to Jacked Up, and I'm teeming with excited energy. I want to find this car. I want to find Spade and see him punished for what he did. Levi parks the car and I'm practically out while the engine's still running. I race up the stairs to the office, then halt. Damn it. He *still* hasn't given me the key. I turn around to find him but he's already there, keys in hands.

"You gotta calm yourself down there, princess," he says.

Jacked Up

"We just need to find this," I say. "And the longer we wait, the harder it will be to find."

He opens the door, and I go straight to the room where the cameras are. He pulls up the feed from earlier today, but goes back too far, to where I'm standing in the back overhearing Grease and Spade. My cheeks flush with embarrassment. I wish I'd never been there. I wish that had never happened. It's mortifying.

But as he forwards past that again, something catches my eye. "Wait!"

Levi freezes, and raises a brow to me. "You see something?"

"Yeah," I say. I lean in closer to the camera. "Look."

While Spade is telling Grease about the fabricated pregnancy, Grease looks over to where I'm crouched by the bush. He knew I was there, the whole time.

"Is Grease in on this, too?" I tell Levi what I suspect, and we look through the footage. Finally we come to the part where Spade told Levi how to find me.

"Zoom in," I tell him. He shows me how, pinching his fingers on the touchscreen. It quickly opens, and on the screen are details for a car exchange program just outside of the city.

"Bingo," I tell him. "They're heading there, I bet."

He nods, looking at the address. "Yep. They'll strip it, take the VIN off, and make sure nothing's identifiable." He shakes his head. "And fuck me, I know that address."

We go to the truck and head to where he took me the day I sent the picture to Spade by accident. When we near it, my skin begins to prickle and my tummy does a weird little flip. Someone's here.

"Stay here and lock the doors," Levi orders. There's nothing from where we sit that in any way indicates there's a stolen car here, but there's danger present and he'll ensure I have no part of it. I sit there and hit the locks when he points to the door and wags his finger at me to remind me to stay put.

Every second that ticks by feels like a minute. I have no idea where he's going or what he's doing, but I hate just sitting here, unable to help in any way. The place is empty and vacant, but when the clouds part, a stream of moonlight filters down, illuminating something on the ground right outside the passenger door of Levi's truck.

A cigar butt.

I go to open the door to yell for Levi but realize in a split second he'd be furious. Plus, that could also alert the thieves we're here. And what does one cigar butt on the ground really mean, anyway?

My hand is still on the door handle when a shadow blocks my vision, and someone's yanking on the door. I scream, and even though he can't reach me I crouch further back in my seat when I see Spade's furious face. He's *right there.* I look wildly around but Levi's nowhere to be seen. Was he hurt? Did someone get to him first?

Spade's glaring at me and yanking on the door handle, but of course it doesn't budge. He's waving his fist and me and it looks like he's cursing up a blue streak. Suddenly, he's yanked from behind and I can't see him at all. He's vanished. Levi's large, furious form dwarfs Spade's smaller frame. Levi tosses him to the ground like he weighs nothing. Spade comes up, fists flying. I scream and cover my face. I can't bear to watch. But quickly, Levi's got the upper hand. He ducks a swing from Spade, then levels Spade with an uppercut to his jaw that knocks Spade clean on his ass. I get up on my knees to peer out the window. Holy shit. Levi's knocked him out cold.

"Call the police back, Tanya," he instructs me, panting. "Call this in. The car's here, and we've got our suspects."

Chapter Sixteen

Levi

It's the day of the car show. Levi's worked his ass off overtime, getting both his car and mine ready for the show, including a few all-nighters. And now it's the day of the show. Yesterday, he showed me my father's car, and it's beautiful. My father's due in from traveling today, and his car's been brought to the show in mint condition.

It looks amazing. God, what that car cost me though.

I lost my dignity, My pride. My arrogance.

My loneliness.

I'm here with Levi, and today I introduce him to my family. I am so beyond caring what they think anymore. I have Levi, and that's what matters.

My father and mother are in the air-conditioned gallery above the main viewing area, where the most expensive seats are. I take Levi by the hand.

"Come on," I tell him. "It's time I introduce you."

There's an hour before his car's on display. We make

our way to the seating area, and when we get there, my mother's ordering champagne and my father's working on what looks like his third martini, as two empty glasses sit by the one he now has.

"Tanya, my love," my father greets, raising his hand.

My mother gives me a cool nod, but her eyes are fixed on the large, muscled, tattooed guy standing next to me who definitely doesn't look like he belongs here.

"Mom, dad, I'd like you to meet Levi."

They both eye me curiously. "I met Levi a few weeks ago, and he's my…" I hesitate. I almost say "daddy," and catch myself just in time. "Boyfriend," I finally finish lamely, my cheeks heating.

My mother shakes his hand first, but my father's giving him a curious look. "How do I know you?' he asks. He tips his head to the side.

"Dad, you might know Levi as Levi DeRocco, the owner of Jacked Up? It's the classic car repair shop."

"Ahh," my father says with a nod. "Now *that* rings a bell. So you've found yourself my competitor, eh?" I know he's joking, but it's something that makes me squirm a little.

"I guess," I say.

"Nice to meet you, Levi," my father says, dismissing him by turning his head away. No guy wearing a leather jacket and tattoos is really worth my father's attention.

"Tanya, did you see someone's brought a '55 Jaguar? It's a beaut," my father says.

I share a quiet smile with Levi. "Yeah, dad. That's actually Levi's."

Now *that's* got my dad's attention.

He turns and he and Levi talk cars until it's time for us to go.

Jacked Up

Levi wins top place in every category there is, and I think I'm even more pleased than he is.

"Congratulations, daddy," I tell him, later that night when we're on his porch swing watching the sun set, crickets chirping lullabies all around us.

"Thank you, princess," he says. He entwines his fingers with mine and smiles. "But I've already got my prize."

Chapter Seventeen

Tanya
Six months later

"Just like that, baby," Levi says. He's standing in front of me at the shop. It's late, the shop's been closed for hours, and he's got every shade pulled down so we're all alone. And it's a damn good thing, because I am completely, 100%, stark naked here on the hood of his car.

He's got his camera, and he's taking what he calls "private shots." After he got the photo shoot from my last gig, he says he's been jonesing for some pictures of "his two favorite girls together." Good thing for him his other girl has an engine and a battery, or I'd have a thing or two to say about that.

After his car won first prize at the show, he's rearranged his shop so that the entire front is set up like a show room, like one might find at a car dealer, but showcasing just one car. Here, the Jaguar is safe, under the lock and key of the shop and the cameras trained on anyone that comes within a foot of it. I work here now, full-time, and I do a helluva lot more than answer phones. I've taken over his marketing, and his business is booming. I'm also doing work on a more personal level.

It was Levi's idea, having me model with cars. He insists I model fully clothed, and I'm fine with that. It's when I pose for him personally that I flash the skin.

"Just like that, baby," he says, prowling around the car with his eyes fixed on me. "Good. Push your arms together and show me what you've got for daddy." I'm getting turned on lying on his car like this, with his eyes fixed on me. That heat in his gaze makes me quiver, and I'm longing for him to touch me.

"Daddy," I whisper. I need him closer. I want him to touch me. I need to feel him.

He puts the camera down. "One more, shot, baby," he says. He walks over to me, and I think he's aiming for a kiss shot, but when he reaches me, he rolls me over on my side, lifts his hand back, and whacks his hand on my ass so hard and loudly, I yelp out loud. Quickly, he picks up the camera and takes a shot.

"There," he says. "A handprint shot. Jesus, that'll be my favorite of the bunch."

"Daddy!" I admonish.

He just shoots me a lewd grin. "Stick that lip out, baby. Just like that. No, deeper, the way that gets you spanked if you do it for real." I stick my tongue out instead. His eyes narrow on me. "Tanya," he warns. "Do it now, or daddy'll spank that bottom for you."

I give him a coy look. I'd like to see him try.

He goes to put the camera down, but I quickly flash him my most winsome grin. "How's that, daddy?'

"God, baby," he groans. He takes six more shots, then puts his camera down and comes to me. "You are so beautiful, love," he says. He's never called me "love" before, and I like it. He calls me princess, baby, babe, honey, sweetheart…but love? That's different.

"You called me love," I say softly. I open my arms to welcome him over to me. He crosses the room with his eyes fixed on me, shrugs out of his leather jacket, then stands front of me in nothing but his shirtsleeves.

"I did, honey," he says, approvingly. "And that's because I love you."

I grin. When he reaches me I tighten my arms around his neck. "And I love you, daddy."

He holds me close.

"You know," he says. "When you were telling me about sitting on that porch swing, and how much you wanted that, I couldn't help but think there was one thing missing."

"Oh yeah?"

"Yeah," he says. "A family. Me, you, the dogs.. and maybe a baby. Or two."

My heart thunders in my chest. I'm strewn across his car naked and he's proposing to me? Is he? Well, for a couple like us, that's probably totally appropriate.

"Yeah?" I croak. The truth is, after the upbringing I've had, I welcome the unconventional like this. It's so totally right being with Levi. I haven't left his side since I met him. Last month, I gave my notice in my apartment, and moved all my things into his place. I love it there. And now, he says he wants me there forever?

He lifts me up into his arms. I wrap my legs around him. He turns around and leans against the hood of the car, then fishes in his pocket. He brings out a black velvet box.

"Marry me, Tanya?"

"Daddy," I breathe. It's a sparkling gem of a diamond set in gold. I smile at him. "Is that a princess cut?" I ask.

"Don't know what the fuck it is," he says with a grin. "Is that a yes?"

"Hmm, let me think about it," I say, tapping my chin.

He growls, takes my mouth with his, then to my shock, slaps my ass so hard I squeal. "Brat," he says, spanking me again.

"Yes!" I yelp out when I can catch my breath. "God, yes I will!"

He groans his approval into my mouth, then turns and lays me on the hood of the car. He makes quick work of removing his shirt.

"Jesus, you're perfect," he whispers in my ear. He fists my long hair in his hand and tugs my head back, then flips me around so I'm splayed belly-down on the hood of his car.

He cups one breast and pinches my nipple and I moan out loud.

"Arch that back, baby," he orders when he unzips his jeans. He's going to fuck me, right here, right on the hood of this car that's been featured in every flashy car magazine from coast to coast. He's going to stake his claim in every way possible and I'm already ready, my body an electric hum of need and want.

"Daddy," I breathe. He holds my hips so hard it hurts, pulling my hair back. I want him hard and unapologetic, so I can feel him inside and out for the rest of the day, and into tomorrow. I feel him at my entrance and hold my breath, waiting for the moment when he marks me. He thrusts in, hard and soft all at once, his grip on me almost painful. Pleasure thunders through me. I writhe beneath him as he rocks his hips, his name on my lips.

"Levi," I groan. "Daddy. I love you."

"And I love you, baby."

He rides me until I climax, ecstasy rolling through me in blissful waves. He groans his own release, holding me tight in my grip until both of us are sated. I'm sweaty and panting, but I look over my shoulder and grin at him. I shoot him a wink.

"I think I need a raise, boss."

THE END

Check out the rest of the Hard n' Dirty books!

Gettin' Dirty by Aubrey Cara
Filthy Fight by Alta Hensley
Hard Wood by Tara Crescent
Blaze by Renee Rose
Hammered by Alexis Alvarez
Drilled by Ava Sinclair
Beauty and the Lumberjacks by Lee Savino

Other books by Jane

What to read next from Jane? Here are some other titles you may enjoy.

Contemporary fiction
Island Captive: A Dark Romance

NYC Doms

Deliverance
Safeguard
Conviction

Masters of Manhattan

Knave

Other books by Jane

Hustler

The Billionaire Daddies

Beauty's Daddy: A Beauty and the Beast Adult Fairy Tale
Mafia Daddy: A Cinderella Adult Fairy Tale
Dungeon Daddy: A Rapunzel Adult Fairy Tale
The Billionaire Daddies boxset

The Boston Doms

My Dom (Boston Doms Book 1)
His Submissive (Boston Doms Book 2)
Her Protector (Boston Doms Book 3)
His Babygirl (Boston Doms Book 4)
His Lady (Boston Doms Book 5)
Her Hero (Boston Doms Book 6)
My Redemption (Boston Doms Book 7)

Other Contemporary Romances

Begin Again (Bound to You Book 1)
Come Back to Me (Bound to You Book 2)
Complete Me (Bound To You Book 3)

Bound to You (Boxed Set)

Other books by Jane

Sunstrokes: Four Hot Tales of Punishment and Pleasure (Anthology)

A Thousand Yesses

Westerns

Her Outlaw Daddy
    Claimed on the Frontier
    Surrendered on the Frontier
    Cowboy Daddies: Two Western Romances

Science Fiction

Aldric: A Sci-Fi Warrior Romance (Heroes of Avalere Book 1)

Idan: A Sci-Fi Warrior Romance (Heroes of Avalere Book 2)

About the Author

USA Today bestselling author Jane Henry pens stern but loving alpha heroes, feisty heroines, and emotion-driven happily-ever-afters. She writes what she loves to read: kink with a tender touch. Jane is a hopeless romantic who lives on the East Coast with a houseful of children and her very own Prince Charming.

You can stalk Jane here!
   The Club (Facebook reader group)
   Website
   Amazon author page
   Goodreads
   Author Facebook page
   Twitter handle: @janehenryauthor
   Instagram

Manufactured by Amazon.ca
Bolton, ON